I0539591

Jay Gets Schooled

by

Ray Smith

First Edition: September 2015

ISBN:9781311219282
ASIN: B014FVDJCK

Published by Ray Smith

Preface:

Please forgive any poor grammar you may find. I could have spent thousands on a professional editor, but then I would probably be in the red forever. I sincerely doubt that I will ever make enough to pay off that kind of editing. I did my best to refresh myself on comma usage and other grammar issues, but I am no professional writer, and I got horrible grades in English classes in school. Several friends have helped me out with that, most notably Bill and Devon.

Disclaimer:

About the adult content:

Contact the author at
ray@raysstories.com
circulatim@gmail.com

Website
Ray's Stories
http://raysstories.com
More books and stories available at the website.

Chapter 1

Jay was a geek. Not a totally lost cause, but surely out of the mainstream. He'd always been thin, tall, and rather dorky. His blue-gray eyes were bright, his sandy-blond hair was heavily curly, and his complexion was fair with the hint of a faded tan. With narrow features and a small chin, he'd been pegged as a dork when he was small. He'd had few friends, and no close ones. He hadn't had someone he considered a best friend since grade school. Now, as a college freshman, he was still alone.

He'd known he was gay at thirteen and had hidden it well. But now, at college, he was working himself up to going to an LGBT meeting. He'd seen several very hot guys attending it, but he could only hurry past the meeting room then retreat.

It'd been almost a month since he'd moved into the dorm, and at first, he had been worried about living in a small room with someone else. Sean, his roommate, had been welcoming and friendly. He was a sophomore who was studying business, but looked more like the jock he also was. When he wasn't studying, Sean was a forward on the school's soccer team and a member of the wrestling team. He was slim, yet buff, and limber. He kept himself remarkably hairless on his chest, under his arms, even his legs. He had straight, dark-brown hair that he kept short, and fine, narrow eyebrows over dark green eyes that stood out powerfully, especially against his moderately tanned complexion. Sean's soft, generous, red lips drew Jay's eyes nearly as much as Sean's firm, round ass. Sean was in great shape, and all the sports had sculpted his buttocks into tight, rounded globes. His legs had also benefited from the activity and were strong and lean. Even though the

1

front of Sean's jockeys were well-stuffed, it was his ass that Jay found most interesting.

In the month since Jay had moved in, Sean had never seen him in anything less than street shorts and a t-shirt. But Sean, being a sophomore, was far less self-conscious about nudity. While he hadn't been naked in front of Sean, he'd more than once removed everything but his jockey shorts while changing or getting ready for bed.

Jay was always careful to not be seen taking peeks at those times, but he did, and never directly, unless they were talking to each other. More than once Jay had been sure that Sean had seen him looking at him while he changed or readied for a shower or bed, yet Sean had never challenged him or said anything.

So far Sean had been open and friendly with Jay; something Jay wasn't familiar with. His few friends back home had been hard-won, but Sean seemed to take to Jay almost instantly. He'd not offered any tours of the campus, or asked him to go out with his friends, or other outright friendly things, but he always said hello when he arrived in their dorm room and always spoke to him in public. He even helped Jay with his classwork on the rare occasions that he needed it.

With a month now under his belt at college, Jay was beginning to feel almost at home. Last weekend, Sean had asked Jay if he could spend the evening out of their dorm room so that Sean could have some privacy for a visitor. His grin made it clear what kind of visitor, and Jay was happy to spend a few hours at the computer lab. He stayed out past the time they had agreed upon, and when he came back, he'd brought a pizza. Sean hadn't volunteered any information about his visitor, and Jay hadn't asked.

Now, on a Friday evening, Sean was out with his teammates, and would be for some time yet. Jay was working on some classwork at the small desk, books open, laptop at hand. Sean was late coming home from soccer practice, but that wasn't surprising. Jay rolled his dark brown eyes under their heavy, dark lashes, and threw down his pencil in frustration. He sat back in the chair and crossed his long arms. The well-worn, solid blue t-shirt was baggy, but as it lay across his form, it revealed his thin chest and nearly concave belly beneath it. An obvious bulge in his sweat-shorts grew more distinct as Jay leaned back in the chair.

Unable to resist any longer, he turned off the radio and opened the browser on his computer. He typed in his favorite website. Nifty didn't have pictures or videos, just stories. Jay loved reading, and the hot stories at Nifty served him well. He found that one of his favorite authors had posted a new chapter in one of his best stories, so he immediately began reading it.

The chapter was short, but hot. Jay read avidly, one hand using the keyboard to forward to the next page, the other tucked into his sweat-shorts, fondling his erection. He stretched his long legs out straight. The blue t-shirt rode upward and revealed his nearly concave belly. A little navel with a few sandy-blond hairs was visible above the waistband of his tan shorts. Just peeking out of the waist of his shorts was a blue elastic waistband.

Both hands now moved to that bulge. He grinned a little more as both of his hands began moving, one tracing the length of his erection, the other cupping the mobile objects below.

Then he heard Sean's key in the door lock. He quickly sat up straight, hiding his lap beneath the desk, closed the browser, and pretended to be deep in study before the door opened.

"Heya, Jay-bo," Sean said as he entered.

"Hi," Jay returned off-handedly.

It was Sean's usual greeting, but delivered in an unusually rounded and curt way. Jay turned and saw Sean's expression.

"What's up? Something wrong?" Jay asked.

"Let's just say…" Sean began as he removed a beer from his backpack, "I was going to get lucky until a few minutes ago."

"Oh? What happened?"

"Nothing I want to talk about," Sean said, opening the beer, then taking a very long drink from it.

Jay watched Sean's throat working, pushing the beverage downward, and wondered if it would look the same if he was swallowing his wad after sucking him off. He quickly pushed the thought away and asked, "Anything you do want to talk about?"

Sean kept swallowing and actually finished the beer before crushing the can in his hand and then tossing it into the trashcan next to his desk. He sat down on his small bed, pulled another from his backpack, then said, "No. Just keep doing your work. I'll live." He opened the beer and drank almost the entire can before stopping to belch.

Jay tried not to think of oral sex as he watched Sean swallow repeatedly. He turned back to his keyboard and tried to get back into his work. Sean turned on the radio, then swung his legs up on his bed and finished the beer.

Jay heard another can being opened. He turned and asked, "You going to get wasted?"

"Very," Sean replied, then asked, "Want one?"

"No, thanks," Jay replied without turning from his keyboard.

Sean drank the beer the same way he had the first two. Jay returned to his work. He managed to finish the lesson and began another. Before he finished that lesson, almost an hour later, Sean had drunk another three beers.

"Out," Sean lamented, tossing the empty can into the trash. Then added, "I'm going to get some more. Want any?"

"Don't drink," Jay answered.

"Too bad," Sean said, then got up and walked toward the door, almost swaying.

Once the door closed, Jay wondered if he had enough time to masturbate before Sean would get back. He began fondling himself, but he found his mind preoccupied with worry about Sean. It was only a couple of blocks to the liquor store, but as drunk as he might be, anything could happen. He ended up sitting at the window, waiting for Sean to come back.

It was only a few minutes before he saw Sean walking back toward the dorm building. Jay went to the restroom at the end of the halls. When he came back, Sean was on his bed, drinking another beer. Sean usually smiled, even to himself, so seeing a frown on his face was a sure sign something was very wrong.

He asked Sean, "You sure there's nothing you want to talk about?"

He hadn't had many friends, but it wasn't because he didn't care to, it was that he had been labeled as a dork in junior high, and had been so worried about being found out as gay that he'd stayed away from making them. Now, Sean was the only person Jay considered a friend, and that something was bothering him was a thorn in his side.

"No," Sean answered, staring at the beer in his hands. "Nothing you'd want to hear."

"How do you know unless you tell me?"

"Just don't worry about it," Sean said firmly, then finished the beer and opened another.

"How many of those can you drink?"

"As many as I can," Sean said, removing another six-pack from his pack.

He downed most of the beer, then belched loudly. He reached for another.

"Guess I'll watch a flick," Jay said, then put on his headphones and turned to his laptop.

As he watched the movie, he also watched Sean. It wasn't long before Sean fell asleep, mostly sitting up on his bed, back against the headboard, beer tilted at a dangerous angle. Jay sat and admired Sean's sleeping form. He was very fit, lean, slightly muscular, slightly tanned. His brown hair was straight, his brows thin and fine, his lashes thick and dark. His face was slightly narrow, his chin rather pointed. Full, lush, red lips stood out clearly. His package also stood out clearly, as he'd slid down somewhat from his sitting position, causing the jeans to ride up.

Sean's erection returned in moments. He fondled it gently as he looked at Sean sleeping, wishing he had the guts to stalk over and fondle Sean's lap instead of merely his own. He knew Sean slept soundly and was almost impossible to wake up by accident. Jay often got up in the middle of the night to use the bathroom, and at first, had been extremely careful not to make any noise. But after a couple of accidents, he'd discovered that it took quite some level of sound to wake him up. After having drunk almost twelve beers, Jay was certain that Sean would sleep through almost anything.

He surprised himself by actually standing up. Still holding his erection, he walked toward Sean. His heart hammered. His erection felt harder than it ever had before as he arrived next to Sean's bed.

It was the most sexually exciting moment of his life. He'd never been so close to someone while excited before, as he thought of sex, never touched himself while so close to someone. And he'd never touched someone else in such a way before.

He held his breath as he leaned down and reached out, then ever so gently placed his hand on Sean's thigh, just an inch below where the sports shorts clung to his package. It was very warm and firm.

He looked up at Sean's face. He was still asleep. This was as close as he'd ever been to him, so he looked closely. In sleep, Sean's face was very relaxed and even smoother than usual. His long, dark lashes stood out. His cheekbones were strong but not sharp. And his large, red, lush lips were parted and moist.

Jay couldn't believe what he was doing. It wasn't like him at all. And he loved it.

Deciding it would make a good cover for what he was doing, and to discern how deeply unconscious Sean was, Jay moved his hand from Sean's thigh then took the beer can from his hand. Sean's fingers relinquished it without resistance, and there was no other reaction from the sleeping Sean. He put the beer on the nightstand, then put his hand back on Sean's thigh.

Jay stood there for long minutes, one hand on Sean's thigh, the other gently fondling his own erection. He looked up at Sean's face often, watching for signs he might be waking. He was so excited that he knew he was going to explode into his shorts soon. His long cock was nearly dancing in his hand through his shorts and underwear. Then, stunned at his own actions, his breath coming in short, rapid gasps, his heart pounding in his chest, he watched his own hand as it slid upward. His fingertips slid beneath the thin material, along Sean's smooth, firm upper thigh.

He couldn't believe what he was feeling. So much warmth! He began gently probing, looking for what was hidden inside the tightly constraining shorts. It was no surprise to find the soft material of Sean's jockey shorts, but it was a bit of a surprise to find such a firmness beneath that. Sean was fully erect.

Then, in the blink of an eye, Jay was suddenly forced onto his back with Sean over him, leering, so close that Jay could smell beer on his breath.

Jay began shaking violently. He hadn't felt so afraid since he'd been bullied back in junior high school. Sean's green eyes continued boring into him, reminding him of past beatings. He liked Sean, considered him a friend, but now that he knew Jay was gay, or at least suspected so, Jay knew that the friendship was over. He briefly wondered if he would end up in the hospital or the morgue. And then he wondered what was involved in changing dorm rooms, if he somehow survived.

Sean was sitting on him and holding both of his arms down firmly on the bed. Sean moved so that he was sitting on Jay's lap, then firmly sat down harder, pressing his buttocks onto Jay's flagging erection. Then he smiled, leaned down, bringing his face closer to Jay's face. Jay tried to push the back of his head into the bed.

"I bet you think about me doing this. And I bet you think about me making you do stuff. Don't you?" Sean asked, nearly close enough to kiss.

Jay stammered a few vowels, unsure of what to say, afraid, but aware that Sean wasn't threatening him in the way he had always been used to.

"I bet you think about me when you jerk it, don't ya?" Sean asked, his face now even closer to Jay's.

More stammered vowels, staccato this time. Jay was nearly paralyzed with fear and shock, but the pressure of Sean's ass on his groin was firing his libido.

"I know what you're like," Sean said softly. "I know what you like. You want someone to take charge. Tell you what to do. How to do it. And make you do it."

Sean's mouth was very close to Jay's now, and Jay had no space left to retreat to. He struggled, but Sean was already completely in control of him.

"I won't make it hurt a lot if you don't try to fight me," Sean said to him, smiling.

"What?" Jay got out before Sean pressed one hand over Jay's mouth as his other hand into Jay's throat. Jay's arms were free, and he pushed both hands against Sean's chest, but he had no chance of pushing him off. He pounded Sean's chest, but Sean just smiled and pushed harder against his throat. He pinned Jay's legs with his ankles and sat with his full weight on Jay's hips. Jay was taller but far slimmer. Sean was stronger and experienced at wrestling.

"Shhh," Sean hissed loudly, as he held Jay in place below him despite Jay's efforts. Sean stared into Jay's eyes. Jay had no choice but to be bared to the bone by Sean's gaze. Sean slid down, now lying on top of Jay, and gyrated his hips over Jay's, grinding his erection into Jay's with force.

"I can gank you out, and fuck you while you're out. I won't like it as much, but… maybe, I might like it more that way." Sean grinned. "I won't have to worry you might scream or something. Hmmm?"

Jay shook his head from side to side violently.

"You want it while you're awake, don't'cha?"

Sean waited for an answer for several seconds, then asked again.

Jay knew Sean was drunk, and apparently very horny, but the idea of him opening a sexual encounter seemed entirely unlikely. Sean had never given any hints that he was interested, or had any experience with guys. Sean had bragged about dating and chasing girls, and his sexual exploits with them.

Yet he could feel Sean's erection grinding into his own.

Jay relented and let his arms fall to his side. His fear was still paramount, but a sexual thrill was growing in his groin as Sean's hardness pressed against his.

"Good boy. Take it like a man, not a little girl. Right? Yeah?"

Jay nodded, both frightened and excited.

"Good," Sean said, pushing his hard dick into Jay's groin with each word, "boy. Gonna, like, this."

Sean shifted his arms in a quick movement, and suddenly he held Jay's hands down on the bed again. Now the smile on Jay's face was no longer hidden under Sean's hand.

Sean smiled wider, then crushed his generous lips onto Jay's. Jay whimpered, but Sean's mouth and tongue smothered it and Sean's own growl of lust. They began gyrating with each other, kissing, Sean nearly crushing Jay's hands with his own.

Sean broke the increasing kisses, then asked, "You're gonna do everything I tell you. Right?"

Jay nodded, grinning.

"Just what I say, and just the way I say. Right?"

Jay nodded.

"You're not gonna make a sound. Not a one. Right?"

Sean squeezed Jay's hands until joints popped.

Jay hissed his breath inward, grinning wider, blushing darker. He nodded.

"It's gonna hurt, and you're gonna take it. Like a man. And silently. Right?"

Jay bit his own smiling lip, then nodded.

"You're gonna take off all my clothes, and you're gonna lick everywhere as the light hits it. Got it? So slow, and kiss it as the light does, or else."

Jay nodded. When Sean released his hands and rolled onto his back, Jay moved so that he could slide the t-shirt upward, kissing side to side, rolling the shirt upward. When Sean's nipples were being licked as well as kissed, Sean slapped the back of Jay's head smartly.

"I didn't say lick anything. That was one. Each one's gonna be harder. Get me?"

"Yes."

Another, harder smack on the back of Jay's head.

"I said silence!" Sean hissed.

Jay nodded, cowed, smiling.

He wasn't sure what he was doing, or what he was getting into, but it was entirely hot and exciting. He liked being told what to do, and he seemed to like the threat of danger and pain.

"Back to work," Sean told him.

Jay obeyed. His pulse raced. His breath came rapidly. He whimpered softly, so softly that Sean couldn't be sure. He couldn't help it. He had never been so turned on before. Not only was there someone else involved, but it was also in a way he had been fantasizing about for some time. It wasn't exactly as he'd dreamed and thought of as he'd jerked himself off, but it was certainly a lot like it.

It was better.

Jay removed one of Sean's arms from the t-shirt, kissing his shoulder and the bare skin under his arm, then the other, and then he pulled it over Sean's head and placed it on the table.

"Now, shoes and socks. And keep using those lips on me as the light hits it."

Jay nodded and did as he was told. He wasn't too into kissing Sean's feet, but being forced to was a huge turn-on. He made sure each toe was kissed before the sock was removed and placed carefully into a shoe. Then the other.

"Now, lay on me."

Sean held the back of Jay's head as they kissed. When Jay let a small groan grow too loud, a sharp crack on the back of his head reminded him to remain quiet. That slap only increased Jay's gyrations against Sean's body below him.

"Now, take off my shorts. And don't touch my dick or balls, or I slap yours. So lay so I can reach 'em."

Jay did as ordered, taking a sixty-nine position on his side next to Sean. Sean massaged his buttocks as Jay kissed his waist. He could smell Sean's groin, and the aroma did something inside of Jay that he instantly loved. His eyes looked longingly at the constrained erection and the bulges below it. Sean's cock was thick and long behind his tight briefs, and it looked to be nearly as long as his own. He loved the length of it, wanted it in his hands, his mouth, and his ass. He wanted to touch it so badly, but he knew it wasn't what Sean wanted. At least, not yet. He wanted more than anything to at least graze it with his nose, but he knew what would come. He didn't like the pain, but he liked being afraid of it. He liked the threat of it. He rolled Sean's shorts down and kissed his thighs, and then down both of Sean's legs as they came out of the shorts.

Sean's hand was massaging Jay's buttocks, but never his groin. Jay's cock was pulsing in slow waves, almost as if he were cumming. His balls ached, too. His whole body felt like his stomach did during an orgasm – tense, charged, quivering. Having someone else caressing his ass was intensely erotic.

"Now, stand over me and take off everything."

Jay did as he was told. When he was down to his briefs, Sean told him to stop. Sean reached up and followed the long arc of Jay's cock several times, end to end. He followed the contours of the ridges on the head, making Jay shiver and his balls rise up high. Then he pulled Jay's briefs down and Jay stepped out of them. Jay's cock was very long and slim. Almost perfectly straight, with subtle edges and a cone-shaped head. His balls were nicely sized, but his tight scrotum was holding them close to his body. His sandy-blond pubic hair was fuzzy but not thick at the base of his long penis, and a slight fuzz was growing on the inside of his thighs.

"Fucking amazing," Sean said admiringly. "I know you're longer than me, but I'll take it all, later. But first, you're gonna

10

take all of mine. Quietly. And without stopping. Now, on your hands and knees over me, sixty-nine style, but don't even breathe on my dick or balls."

Once Jay was in place over him, Sean wrapped Jay's underwear around two fingers, spat on the tip of the cloth covering his fingers, and then wiped Jay's pink hole with them.

"This is now mine," Sean said. "No one else can touch it. Not even yourself. Not even when you're alone. Understand?"

Jay nodded. Sean finished with the briefs, then attacked Jay's ass with his tongue. Jay fought back gasps and groans as Sean's tongue licked and probed his anus. He could feel Sean spitting through his hole, into him. He could feel Sean's tongue pushing its way into him. Soon, Sean was pushing a finger into him.

"So, my finger's not the first thing in you, is it?"

"No," Jay admitted with a snicker.

A sharp slap to Jay's dangling balls reminded him to remain quiet. That was followed by three fingers forcing their way into him. He bit back a yell of pain, allowing only a small grunt to escape.

"I'll let that one pass," Sean said.

He told Jay to remove his briefs with his teeth, but not to touch his cock or balls in any way. That took considerable care and time. Tim Sean spent gliding his three fingers into and out of Jay's loosening circle. Once the white briefs were gone, Sean's long, thick cock lay on his belly, reaching up nearly to his navel.

Jay stared at it, admiring it, wanting badly to at least touch it, though he ached to take it into his mouth. The aroma was making him salivate. It was at least seven inches long, curved a little to the left. The hair at the base was brown and thick. The head was prominent and heavily ridged, and with a large, oval, open hole in the tip. The balls hung low and were large, and the brown hairs showed up clearly against the white skin. Very little hair surrounded his privates or grew on his muscular yet lean thighs.

Sean spat onto his fingers and then moved them deeply into Jay's pink sphincter. Jay tried not to groan as those fingers found a sensitive place and began massaging it. He had never felt anything quite like it before. He had to fight the urge to groan and moan with all his concentration.

Jay's cock jumped, then a string of pre-cum dangled from it. Jay felt as if he sneezed he would blow off a wad so large he would end up with a rupture.

"On your back."

Jay complied. Sean pushed his cock against Jay's lips. Jay opened his mouth and moved his head forward to take the cock, but Sean pulled it back.

"Only the tip. Only the head. Go past it..." Sean warned vaguely, raising a hand.

Jay nodded, then followed the directions. Finally, Jay felt a cock in his mouth that wasn't his own. The taste made his saliva flow freely. He moved his tongue around the thick head and began applying suction.

"Suck, and suck like your balls depended on it!" Sean said firmly, as he gave a firm squeeze to Jay's balls. "Ah! Yes!"

Sean moved his head in and out of Jay's lips, groaning and giving directions. He played with Jay's cock and balls, but never stroked it or touched the head. Jay gyrated wildly.

"You've got the biggest dick I've ever seen. How long is it?" Sean asked.

Jay was unsure whether to speak until Jay slapped his balls after pulling his dick from his mouth.

"Eight inches and three quarters."

"Serious?"

Jay nodded.

"Fuck! What a cock! When did it get so huge?"

Jay turned scarlet and grinned.

"When?" Sean asked again, then slapped Jay's balls again, harder.

"When I was thirteen. It started growing. Just got long."

"Monster! And I will take all of it. Every last inch. But first, you gotta take mine."

Sean pulled his cock's head out of Jay's mouth, made Jay roll onto his front, then slid down the bed until he could spit into Jay's ass. Then he began licking it.

Another new, awesome sensation flashed through Jay's nerves. It took all of his concentration to remember to remain silent despite the nearly overwhelming urge to groan, moan, and even laugh.

Then Sean began sliding three fingers in and out of it.

Nearly every thrust brought that intense internal thrill of his prostate being bumped.

After at least a full minute, Sean told Jay to roll over, then he took Jay's long cock-head into his mouth and licked every centimeter of it. He never sucked. Jay still shuddered with the pleasure of someone else's tongue lashing his sensitive head.

After a minute or so, Sean said, "It's time. Sit on my cock and take it all. Like a man. Now!"

Jay positioned himself over Sean's hips, positioned Sean's cock against his quivering hole, and began to impale himself on it. It was his first time, and somewhat awkward, but Jay had put other things in himself before. Within a couple of moments, Jay was sweating as he hovered over Sean and forced the thick hardness into himself.

It hurt, and Jay did all he could to remain silent, but Sean was urging him downward sooner than he was comfortable with. The pain and pressure in that sensitive area were overwhelming Jay, and he was frightened as well as incredibly turned on. His whole body thrummed with the intensity of the moment.

When Sean placed his hands on Jay's thighs and pulled him down while he thrust upward, Jay squealed. Sean slapped his hanging balls sharply, making Jay jolt in pain.

Sean pushed upward and pulled Jay downward. Jay had never had anything so thick in him before, and it was all he could do not to cry out. He was covered with sweat and shaking as the cheeks of his ass finally came to rest on Sean's hips.

"Good boy. Now ride me."

Jay raised himself, then dropped down. He began moving up and down in a regular motion, almost panting. What little pain had existed at first was now pleasure. Sean demanded more speed. Jay moved faster.

"Not enough!" Sean said, then threw Jay over on his side then rolled Jay onto his back.

He pushed Jay's legs up, knees against his chest, spat onto and into him. He then spat several times onto his own cock head, then he positioned himself. He pushed his cock all the way into Jay in one movement. Jay groaned in pain, and again when Sean slapped his face.

"Quiet!"

Sean began thrusting, quickly and deeply. He groaned softly with each thrust, pressing Jay's legs into his chest, constricting his breathing. Often, Jay's balls were crushed by Sean's powerful thrusts. That pain was exquisitely intense. The sound of slapping skin drowned out Jay's little whimpers. Both of them were sweating and panting now.

"Oh, fuck, yes! Nice ass! Oh, fuck, ain't, gonna, be, long! Fuck!"

Faster and faster, Sean pounded Jay, forcing a small grunt out of Jay with each crushing thrust. Especially when his balls were slammed by Sean's efforts. Jay could feel the hot, yielding mass of Sean's cock moving through his rectum. It was better than he had imagined. It filled and emptied him, thrilling him to his core. His cock twitched and pulsed, leaking pre-cum that dripped into his navel.

"Oh, fuck, yes! Oh, man, I'm gonna, fill, you, up! Yes!"

Sean began repeating, "Yes!" with each breath and thrust. Then, "Fuck!" and he pushed all the way inside of Jay, held there trembling, and groaned out a long, slow groan as he pumped his semen into Jay, his cock spasming violently.

Jay felt Sean's cock pumping inside of him. It felt as if this was the real reason for the existence of his anus, this was what it was really for. The warm wetness spreading inside of him seemed to be more than possible for one person to ejaculate. Sean's little movements as he came sent waves of pleasure through Jay's entire body.

Jay watched as Sean's eyes rolled upward, his lips parted in a grimace of ecstasy as his face turned red. He had never seen another guy cum in person before, and watching Sean's attractive features convulsed in an orgasm nearly put Jay into his own final approach.

The swelling of his cock was painful now. His balls hurt, actually hurt, and his rectum hurt with Sean's thick, hard cock still throbbing as it finished pumping his hot semen into him.

When Sean stopped moving, then opened his eyes, Jay was smiling up at him. Sean stretched down and kissed him powerfully.

When Sean pulled himself from inside of Jay, he let his legs straighten out with a groan of pain at their aches. He flinched, waiting for the slap. Instead, Sean took one of Jay's balls into each of his hands, then grinned at Jay.

Jay trembled, waiting for the pain he knew was coming, that he deserved. It came, and Sean grinned. Jay smiled as he grimaced. Then Sean began stroking Jay's long cock with both of his hands. In only seconds, Jay felt his body tensing and the waves of release building up beneath his balls.

Jay opened his mouth to say so, but remembered his instructions and bit it back. Sean knew what he was going to say.

Sean slammed his hands down to the base of Jay's cock just as it began jerking, and held them there, pulling the skin back tightly, almost painfully.

"OH GOD!" Jay grunted behind his teeth as his back arched.

Jay's cock felt as if it were ripping open from the inside outward as his balls pushed through his urethra. As he pumped his hot semen onto another's hands for the first time, Jay lost his breath. His eyes closed tightly, his lips curled, his body tensed, and joints popped. Wave after wave of powerful pulses throbbed through his cock as his semen flew in high arcs to land in long strings from his chin to his pubic hair.

Finally, he collapsed. He struggled to pull away as Sean's tongue began cleaning him up, but Sean held his cock, licking all over it, driving Jay into convulsions.

"Please!" Jay begged, knowing it wouldn't do any good, but unable not to.

Sean slapped his balls again, making Jay shudder once. Then Sean slid his lips over Jay's hot, sensitive head, and sucked him for the first time. Jay had never felt anything like it. He had been sucking his own head for some time, but was only able to get just the head into his own mouth. The suction he gave himself had felt very good, but what Sean was doing to him now was many times as pleasurable.

It went on forever to Jay. He needed Sean to stop, but he wouldn't. The sensations were growing so powerful that Jay was afraid he would pass out. Tension rose from between his thighs and seemed to rob him of breath and strength.

It felt as if it went on for hours. He was spent, exhausted, cramping, but Sean kept sucking and licking, bobbing up and down, and stroking his long cock.

It became bearable, but barely. And it went on. And on. Jay felt as if he had been in bed with Sean for days. His body felt as if he were drained of blood and merely alive on will alone. Only the extreme pleasure kept him alive.

Sean was sucking Jay's head and stroking his long cock loosely with both hands, running over the edges of his head, when Jay hissed, "Sean! OH, GOD DAMN!"

Jay felt an orgasm coming that was already robbing him of the ability to control his breathing. He had never been given head before, other than his own attempts, and having his first blow-job come directly after the first orgasm he had ever had with someone else was so intense that he began to feel as if he were separating from his body.

The pressure built further, causing Jay's legs to run in place. He was sweating profusely and his entire body began to convulse. Sean felt Jay's cum slam into the back of his throat with so much force it made him cough. He lost the rest of the hot cum as he moved away to cough and clear his throat. Jet after jet of white fired into the air, arced, and landed on Jay's belly with audible slaps.

Jay's breath caught in his throat, his pulse pounded in his ears and his cock. The orgasm pulled his body apart and sent waves through him that halted his breath and wracked his muscles.

Suddenly, Jay gasped, and fell limp like a rag doll, panting and sweating and shaking.

"You're not done. I want off again, right now. And you'll swallow it all. Miss a drop and I hurt you."

Sean slid up Jay's body, straddling him, then slid his cock into Jay's mouth. Jay took it despite the smell and taste of his own ass, and worked it as Sean instructed him. It was almost impossible to do what Sean demanded. He was panting for breath, and having Sean's long, thick cock in his mouth hindered his breathing. But he did as he was told. When he was told to, he cupped Sean's balls, massaged them, licked and sucked at Sean's head, and used his tongue as commanded.

For long minutes Sean thrust his long cock in and out of Jay's mouth. The taste of his own ass faded, replaced by Sean's cock and pre-cum. That made Jay suck and lick all that much harder. He loved the taste of Sean's cock and his pre-cum, and couldn't wait for the hot cum.

"Take it all! Every last fucking drop! One spilled drop out

of your lips and I crush one of these!"

Sean grabbed Jay's balls and squeezed them tightly.

Sean's cock swelled and jerked in Jay's mouth, and without warning, Sean shoved himself all the way into Jay's mouth, and into his throat, gagging him. Sean didn't relent, and his cum rolled down the back of Jay's throat as Jay gagged and coughed some cum out through his nose.

Jay did his best, but some white drips formed at the corners of his mouth along with the streams from his nose. He was still coughing through his nose, doing his best not to do so into Sean's cock, or to suffocate.

To Jay, it seemed to go on forever. The hot, thick cum filled his mouth and nose with their taste and smell. It was hard to breathe with the heavy stuff clogging his nose and the back of his throat. Pulse after pulse of hot cum filled his throat and Jay struggled not to gag, and to breathe. He managed to swallow, finally, and he could feel Sean's thickness in his throat as it worked around it.

"Oh, man! That's it! All of it!" Sean cried.

Gagging still, the thick cum in his nose and nasal passages, Jay learned to work his throat around a hard cock in it.

"That's it! That's how you do it!" Sean grunted as his body shuddered at the sensation of Jay's throat muscles working around his ejaculating head.

Then his orgasm waned, and he demanded, "Clean me up!"

Jay licked, sucked, and swallowed, trying to breathe, too. Sean pulled his cock from Jay's mouth and lay down on top of him. The two young men smiling at each other. Once Jay was breathing smoothly, Sean kissed him.

"You okay now?"

Jay nodded, a grin returning to his lips.

"Was it too rough?"

Jay shook his head, still grinning.

"Good. Then can we do this again?"

Jay nodded and snickered, blushing darker.

"Good. You are not allowed to jerk off. Period." Sean grabbed Jay's balls and gently squeezed them. "Or else. Understand?"

Jay smiled and nodded.

"You can talk now."

"Thank you," Jay said. He saw that Sean's smile wavered a

little, and he wondered why, until it occurred to him what he had forgotten. "Master."

"Good boy. Tomorrow night, wear clothes you won't mind losing, and shower really well. Now, get some sleep. You're gonna need your energy tomorrow."

"Yes, sir."

Sean kissed him once, quickly, then sat up beside him.

"Get in your own bed. But you'd better blow your nose and clean up, first."

Jay gathered his clothes, then went to his bed. His nose was full of Sean's cum, and it took a lot of blowing to clear it out. He used wet-wipes on his face after licking his lips clean first.

Meanwhile, Sean cleaned himself with paper towel then wet-wipes.

They watched each other the entire time.

Sean was glad he had a new slave, and one that wasn't experienced, and one that was so willing.

Jay was overjoyed he had his first lover. His first master.

Both were smiling and happy, enjoying the sights.

When they were clean, Sean walked to the light switch. Jay watched him every step, admiring every inch of his body. Sean paused, smiling at Jay, letting him get a good look, then turned off the lights.

It had been awesome. Not exactly as he'd dreamed or fantasized, but better in some ways. He wondered if Sean would ever stay in the bed with him overnight. He wanted to feel his strong arms around him all night. He ached to find out what that was like. At least now he knew what it was like to be with someone. To be owned.

It was wonderful.

Chapter 2

It was almost eight p.m., Sean was still out with his friends, and Jay was pacing the floor of their dorm room.

He'd never had many friends, so it had been easy to be alone before. But now, he ached for Sean's company. He couldn't stand being alone.

Sean had acted normally when they woke up, as if nothing had happened. Sean had gotten out of his bed, pulled on his shorts from last night, gathered clean clothes, then headed to the shower. All without a sign of what had happened last night. When he'd come back, Jay was dressed, and Sean said he was going to soccer practice and would be back at the usual time after hanging out with his friends. Just as he'd done before.

They had seen each other when Jay went out for lunch, passing each other near the edge of campus. Sean had given him the usual nod and, "Hey," then one quick, leering grin as they passed. He hadn't really expected anything different, but he knew now that he had hoped for something different.

Jay's ass was still a little sore. He had used his finger in himself before, until he had found a smooth-handled screwdriver that he had used ever since, but it wasn't the same size as a real dick. It certainly hadn't prepared him for Sean's large, thick dick. And it couldn't have prepared him for taking Sean's large dick as quickly and forcefully as Sean had made him take it. Even his bowel movement last night, hours later, had hurt. And his penis was slightly sore as well when it swelled up at the memories of last night.

Sean had told him that he couldn't masturbate. He ached to, but denying himself on orders was a huge turn-on. And Sean had said that his ass now belonged to him. That was exciting, too.

He had gotten ready for Sean by changing into old jeans, a shirt, and a pair of blue briefs, none of which he would miss, as Sean had ordered last night. He'd had a thorough shower, also as Sean had ordered.

He adjusted his erection yet again. It had been nearly constant since waking up that morning. He checked himself out in the mirror again.

The tall, skinny, geeky guy he saw in it made him grimace, as usual. He'd always wanted someone to take an interest in him sexually, and he'd always liked guys like Sean and other jocks, but he had never really expected anyone like them to ever be interested in him. The idea of Sean liking him enough to have sex with him still seemed impossible. The fact that Sean even knew his dark secret was even more impossible. He had no idea how Sean could have possibly known about his desire, almost need, to be afraid and controlled. He had only recently discovered it himself.

As he waited for Sean to arrive, he was anxious, nervous, and impatient. He couldn't wait for another session with Sean. The fear of what Sean would do to him made his heart race and his breath come quickly. The prospect of sex was more than enough to excite him, of course, but knowing that Sean knew about his particular sexual need made the anticipation almost unbearable.

He rubbed his groin, running his hand along his long erection, making himself sigh deeply. He had never felt so charged up and ready for sex before in his life. He couldn't wait.

At the sound of keys in the door, Jay almost jumped out of his skin. He hurriedly sat at his desk and tried to look nonchalant.

"Jay," Sean said as he walked in.

"Sean."

Both grinned, while Jay also reddened deeply. Sean was wearing tight jeans and a tight, black shirt. They showed off his body and his huge package well.

"You know why I didn't talk to you today, right?"

"I think so. I mean, this don't mean we're friends or anything."

"I knew you'd think that," Sean said as he locked the door. "But, you're wrong."

Jay's face now wore a confused expression.

Sean sat on his own bed.

"Good. Look, well, look. I wanna talk to you, okay?"

"Sure," Jay replied, curious, hoping that Sean wasn't about to tell him that last night had been a mistake.

"We can't act differently around campus, be buddies or something, because we never have before. It would look funny. Raise suspicions. Get questions being asked."

Jay nodded as Sean talked. He liked how Sean looked. His dark-brown hair was always neat. He was shorter than Jay, but then most guys were. His dark-green eyes under his dark brows and lashes glowed, as always, standing out against his tanned face. Jay almost found it hard to hear Sean's words, having to concentrate to keep his mind on listening instead of soaking in Sean's beauty.

"So, around campus, we're the same as before, okay?"

Jay nodded, confused. He didn't understand what Sean was saying until Sean put it forward simply.

"I like you, Jay. Your eyes are something, man. So deep and soft a brown, and you've got that great, curly, blond hair. And, well, I don't know why, but I always liked tall guys. I mean…"

Sean sighed and grinned at Jay. Jay grinned back, starting to understand.

"I, just like you. And, I want, I want to be friends, okay? But, not boyfriends. Get me?"

Jay nodded, turning redder, his grin growing wider.

"So, we stay friends, okay?"

Jay nodded more.

"I want to, so you can trust me. Okay?"

Jay nodded more.

"You can talk. I didn't say you couldn't. When we're not messing around and shit, just be normal, okay?"

Jay laughed, then said, "I know. I just… I'm not sure what to say."

"Are you okay with being friends?"

Jay nodded vigorously, ginning widely, blushing violently.

"See, if we're friends, and we trust each other, there's things we can do."

"Like what?" Jay asked happily.

"Oh, don't ask. You'll see," Sean said, grinning lopsidedly.

That grin did things to Jay he had never felt before. He liked it.

"I have a couple of questions," Sean said, patting the bed next to him.

Jay stood up and joined him on his bed. Sean scooted closer to him, making Jay's heart beat harder and faster.

"I've seen how you act and stuff, so I know you like being told what to do. I knew that easy. But, what I don't know, is, how much you like being hurt. You didn't do anything to make me hurt you yesterday. You just like being bossed?"

Jay nodded, turning red.

"You can talk," Sean reminded him.

"I know. I…" he sighed deeply. "I just, don't know what to answer. I mean, uh, no, I don't think I like being hurt."

"So, you just like being told what to do?"

Jay nodded, then said, "Sorta, like, being, you know… not knowing if I'm gonna be hurt, I guess."

"Ah, you like being scared," Jay said, his eyes lighting up.

Jay nodded shyly.

"You like being worried you'll get hurt."

Jay shrugged, grinning wide, looking like an embarrassed child.

"So that way I know what you like. So I can give it to you. See?"

Jay nodded, again blushing furiously. Sean grinned and picked up his overnight bag. He pulled a pair of handcuffs out and held them up with a questioning grin. Jay grinned and smiled, then held out his hands together. His erection pulsed in reaction, and the rest of his body joined in the excitement. Sean applied the handcuffs, being careful not to over tighten them, even asking if they were too tight.

"Now, I want you to know what I like, so you can give it to me, okay?"

"I want to give you what you want," Jay said excitedly.

Sean leaned in close, then kissed him. Jay's dick began throbbing, and he almost melted into Sean's arms. Sean pulled them down so that they were laying on the bed on their sides, kissing, Sean's hands exploring. Soon Sean was laying over Jay, nearly holding him down as he had done yesterday. Sean ground his crotch into Jay's again and again as they kissed and Sean's hands roamed over Jay's shivering body.

Eventually, Sean pulled away and continued, "I like telling someone what to do. Control. Power. I'll be honest... I love bossing my slave around."

Sean adjusted his position, making sure that Jay was under him, totally. Sean moved so that one thigh was in Jay's groin, and then he jerked that leg upward, into Jay's balls.

Jay groaned and gasped.

Sean took hold of the short chain between the cuffs and pulled them until Jay's arms were above his head in an awkward and nearly painful position. There, he removed one cuff and passed it through the headboard of the bed, then put it back on Jay's wrist.

"I love to hurt my slave. Make him whine and beg me to stop hurting him. I love it when my slave cries in pain and sweats from it."

Jay's grin flattened.

Sean pulled a little red ball on a strap from his overnight bag. Jay began to wonder if he had bitten off more than he could chew, as Sean inserted the ball into his mouth and buckled the strap, tightening it down. The excitement was still high, but Jay was also starting to worry a little.

"Not too tight?" Sean asked.

Jay shook his head, some of the worry abated by Sean's concern. Sean turned back to the little bag and pulled out another object. This one sent shivers through Jay. The dildo was far larger than even his own dick, and he knew without a doubt that it would hurt no matter how carefully it was inserted. He began to sweat. There was no hint of any smile in his eyes now, only fear.

Despite the fear, or maybe because of it, Jay felt his cock throbbing. His entire body felt as if little fires were licking along his nerves. He shivered faintly. He saw Sean look at the clock.

"Now, like I said, I like hurting my slave. I like being in charge, and making my slave hurt."

Sean laid the dildo on the bed next to Jay, then patted it.

"Dexter here has hurt before. He's made me very happy before."

Now Sean removed a jar of Vaseline from the bag, then he

got a roll of paper towels. Next, Sean removed gauze pads and tape from the overnight bag. Jay worried that he knew what the bandages were for. He began to sweat more, and the shakes were no longer just from the anticipation of sexual fulfillment.

Jay pulled on the handcuffs, hoping that they were fake and he could easily break the chain between them. He struggled as Sean laughed softly and removed his shoes.

"They're real," Sean said as he began pulling Jay's socks off his feet. "You can struggle. I like that."

Once Jay's socks were off, Sean sat on his legs, running his hand under Jay's shirt and running them over his stomach and chest for a few moments, smiling down at Jay.

Sean reached back into his bag. This time he pulled out another pair of cuffs and a black rubber strap with metal hooks on both ends. He manhandled Jay into laying lengthwise on the bed and put the cuffs on Jay's ankles. He then passed one hook through the chain between the cuffs, then he wrapped the other end around the bedpost. Jay was fully restrained, stretched out straight on his back.

"Now, Jay, don't struggle so much. I won't hurt you... too much. I don't have to use the dildo today, if you cooperate, so you can relax."

He glanced at the clock, then sat on Jay's legs, unfastened Jay's jeans, then shoved his hand into his underwear.

"Sorta hard, but not all the way. Afraid?"

Jay nodded vigorously.

"Jay, listen to me close," Sean said, bending down so that his nose was touching Jay's. "Listen to me. Close. I won't hurt you. Not for real. Maybe a little, for the fun, but nothing for real. This is for fun. Enjoy it. I promise, *promise*, that I won't go too far. I won't really hurt you. I will only hurt you enough to make it fun. Do you get it?"

Jay seemed to relax, at least he stopped struggling as much.

"Good. Listen to me. I know you don't like pain, but I'm going to cause you some. So that you know the threat is real. So you know there will be pain if you don't do just as I say. You understand?"

Jay nodded hesitantly.

"Good. I won't really hurt you. Not bad. Just if you don't do what I say. If you don't, I'll hurt you. But only then. So do what I say, and you won't feel any real pain."

Sean twisted one of Jay's nipples, more than enough to hurt him. Jay winced and grimaced.

"Not too much?"

Jay shook his head slowly.

"Good."

Sean twisted the other nipple with more force. Jay arced his back and clamped his eyes closed in a grimace of pain, nearly growling through the gag.

"Too much?"

Jay nodded.

"Good to know. Now, like I said, I'm not going to hurt you a lot. Some guys like that. Some guys like pain, and a lot of it. But you don't, so I won't do that. What you like is the threat of it. Being scared of it. So I have to give you some pain, so you know I will if you don't do what I say. Understand?"

Jay nodded. It was what he wanted, and what he thought he liked, but he wasn't sure.

"Good."

Sean slapped him.

"Now, remember that. That wasn't hard. I'll give you much more than that if you don't' listen to me and do exactly what I say. Understand?"

Before Jay could answer, Sean slapped him again, harder. Jay nodded.

Jay wasn't sure this was what he wanted. It was frightening, and he kind of liked that, but he wasn't enjoying it as much as he hoped he would, or as much as he had the things they'd done last night.

"Now that you can't struggle, I want to tell you something else. See, I lied. I do love hurting my slave, but I don't care if you like pain or not. I'm going to hurt you as much as I want to. And you're going to get hard, and you're going to fuck me, or I'm going to hurt you so bad!"

Sean slapped him again, this time bringing tears to Jay's eyes.

"Now, if I were you, I'd close my eyes and think dirty thoughts, and get me a nice, hard dick to sit on, or you're gonna see what pain is all about. Hear me?"

Sean slapped him again. Jay nodded.

Sean checked the clock, then reached into his pack again,

this time removing a pocket knife. Jay's eyes widened, and he started sweating. He pulled at the cuffs on his hands and ankles, but they didn't give an inch. Now Jay truly began to worry.

"This little puppy is so sharp, I could cut your ball sack and you won't feel it until I rub the Ben Gay into it."

Sean smiled down at Jay as he opened the knife.

"Oh, yeah, I brought it," Sean said threateningly, then removed a large tube from his pack.

Jay swallowed. This was far more than he had hoped for, and now he regretted it. He had always known that he was a nobody to people like Sean.

Sean put the tube down, then moved off of Jay's legs. He slid the knife under the cuff of Jay's jeans and began sawing through them. Soon he was sliding the knife up Jay's legs, cutting through the leg of the jeans.

The cold steel on the back of the knife blade slid along Jay's thigh, making him shudder. As it slid along his hip, he held his breath. When the knife came to the waistband, Sean sawed through it forcefully. Soon the other pants leg was slit, and the jeans were tugged forcefully away and thrown aside.

Jay's erection had softened with his fear. Sean massaged it, playing with it, and his balls with his other hand. Sean placed the tip of the knife between the leg seam of Jay's briefs and his skin. He began slowly moving the blade back and forth, slowly cutting through the material, the dull side of the blade rubbing against Jay's tender skin dangerously close to his erection.

Jay shivered and stretched upward in ecstasy, careful not to move too much and put himself at risk.

Sean cut through the leg-band of the briefs, then slid the knife sideways, the back of the blade sliding along the sensitive skin behind his balls. Then Sean started on the other leg seam. He grinned when Jay whimpered softly as the blade scratched Jay's skin. When that leg-band gave, the front half of the briefs flapped upward, letting the eight-plus inches of Jay's dick pop free and his balls drop free of the constraint of the briefs.

"Damn, Jay, you got the meat!" Sean said with glee. "I usually don't like being hurt, but I think I'm gonna love being hurt by this monster!"

Sean wrapped his hand around Jay's cock and squeezed it. Even before then, pre-cum had gathered at the hole, but now a trail of it formed as a large, clear bead of the fluid rolled down the top of the head. Sean trapped it, wiped it up, and placed it into his mouth. Sean smiled around his fingers.

"Mmmm, so good," he sighed. "I want more. I'm gonna get it, too. If I have to keep you tied up all week, I'm gonna get as much of that as I can get."

Sean pulled Jay's shirt up by the tail and began cutting upward. Once he cut through the neck, he pushed the two halves apart, then put the knife on the table and picked up the dildo. He traced the tip of it along Jay's brow and down along his cheek. Jay shivered.

"You know Dexter here wants in you, right?"

Jay nodded.

"You know it's gonna hurt, don't you?"

Jay nodded, his eyes widening a little.

"Do you want Dexter inside you?"

Jay didn't respond. He wasn't sure if he did or not. He wanted fucked again, like yesterday, but not by something so huge. It had been all he could do to take Sean's dick, but the dildo was large enough to certainly hurt, no matter how slowly and carefully it was inserted.

Jay shook his head.

"Then there's one way to keep Dexter from splitting you wide open. And that's if you fuck me right, just the way I want, and don't cum until I do. Understand?"

Jay nodded.

Sean nodded and grinned. He checked the clock, then picked up the Vaseline from the table. He applied some to the tip and middle of Dexter, then turned around so that his back was to Jay, and told him to spread his legs. Jay did, as far as he could with his ankles cuffed to the bed frame. Sean pressed the tip of Dexter to the crack below Jay's ball sack, then nestled Dexter up against Jay's hole.

"Now, if you can't or don't give me what I want just as I want it, Dexter is gonna get what he wants."

Sean stood up on the bed, straddling Jay. He took his shirt off and threw it aside. Then he removed his jeans and threw them to the side. The sight of Sean's long, hard dick pushing against his briefs made Jay's dick dance in reaction. Then, as slowly as a strip-tease artist, he slid his underwear down his legs. His long erection stood out proudly, aimed just a little upward from horizontal. His balls hung low.

There was a knock on the door.

Jay jerked violently against the cuffs. Sean grinned widely.

"Don't worry, I'll get it," Sean said, stepping down to the floor.

Sean watched Jay's struggles as he walked slowly toward the door. He struggled fiercely against the cuffs, but there was no use. He was horrified. He wasn't sure who it could be. Sean had quite a few friends, but none of them ever came over without calling first – Sean could be anywhere at any time. Whoever it was, Sean answering the door with him tied up naked on the bed was a nightmare.

Sean laughed, then went to his overnight bag and pulled out a large black cloth. He shook it open, and Jay saw that it was a hood. He struggled as Sean slid it on over his head. He shivered in horror, fear, dread, and shame.

Then he heard the door lock, and then the door opening. Jay nearly fainted.

Sean and the someone laughed. Jay felt his entire body blush and his erection shrinking. He began to wonder what was going on when he felt the bed move and heard what sounded like kissing.

Hands roamed over his body. More than two. They touched him everywhere. His erection returned as he realized he wasn't being beaten, and that the four hands were eager and willing. He became hugely turned on.

Again, Jay was torn. He liked Sean, a lot, but having him sitting on his bed with someone, he didn't know who, feeling his body, was bizarre. He wanted Sean, but to himself, not to share with someone else.

Jay jerked in surprise when the hood was ripped away. He blinked, then saw that the other boy was one of Sean's friends, Billy. He wasn't bad looking, but Jay wasn't all that attracted to him. Well, he was, somewhat, but nothing like he was attracted to Sean. Billy was another jock who had always ignored Jay, and was even stronger and buffer than Sean. His red hair wasn't great as far as Jay was concerned, either. And Jay didn't care for Billy's gray eyes, freckles, or pale complexion.

But obviously, that wasn't going to matter, and Jay knew it.

The boys ignored Jay as they kissed and Sean stripped Billy naked. Billy's body was thick and sturdy, with muscles everywhere. His chest was pale and smooth, with large, pink nipples. His abdomen was smooth, but contoured by muscle. His pubic hair was bright red. His cock wasn't very long, likely less than six inches, but rather thick with a very bulbous head. Veins traced wandering paths around the pale and pink shaft. His sack was very pink and held two very large balls that hung down far from his body.

They kissed and played with each other as if Jay wasn't there. Jay's dick began throbbing its way back to harness as he watched them. They lay down and continued kissing and touching each other, next to Jay, ignoring him.

It began to drive Jay crazy. He could clearly see every inch of them both as they explored each other. When they turned so that they could sixty-nine each other, and began doing so, Jay's cock began to drip pre-cum into his navel.

Billy was upside down to Jay, and Jay could see between the cheeks of his ass and under and behind his balls, places Jay had never seen on another guy before. That made his cock jump and twitch, and drool more pre-cum into his navel. His body trembled.

He had a clear view as Sean's fingers spread Billy's pale cheeks. He was smooth there, and very pale. Sean's middle finger circled the pink pucker several times before it entered it. Jay's dick danced on his belly, his breath coming faster, his entire body now trembling with lust.

Jay could see Sean's face below Billy's groin, and Billy's cock sliding in and out of Sean's mouth. Billy's balls hung low, and were fairly large, obscuring the view of Sean's face a little.

He watched as Sean fingered Billy, then pushed a second finger in, spreading Billy's hole. Billy's groans, and Sean's, sent waves of pleasure through Jay's body. He wanted to do what Sean was doing, or what Billy was, anything but lay there cuffed, stationary, unable to have fun too.

"How about we get started?" Sean asked.

Billy got up, allowing Sean up as well. They both looked at Jay.

"So, you think he's ready to join us?" Billy asked.

"I don't know for sure. I know he likes being told what to do, and he likes being afraid of being hurt. He don't mind some hurt, too, but not much."

"Ah, a lightweight, huh? Well, I think I can handle that. So, what do we do with him?"

"Well, I think you should sit on his face, while I sit on his dick. For starters."

"Sounds great!" Billy said enthusiastically, then removed the ball from Jay's mouth. He swung one leg over Jay's face and sat down forcefully, facing Sean as Sean sat down on Jay's hips facing Billy. Billy said, "Now, I want to feel that tongue working like crazy. And if I don't like what you're doin', I'll ask Sean to punish you."

Jay could smell Billy's body, and his ass, and it wasn't so bad. In a way, it was almost as pleasant as Sean's smells yesterday. Jay only wished it was Sean on his face, not Billy. He sighed as he felt Sean smearing his cock with Vaseline. He was using just two fingers, making sure to excite Jay as little as possible. He applied it quickly, too.

"I don't feel anything," Billy said, a warning clear in his tone.

Jay grunted when Sean slapped his balls. He stuck his tongue out and directly into Billy's hole. He began to lick around it. It wasn't so bad, and was obviously very clean, and soon Jay found himself enjoying it. He moved his tongue in circles and poked it into Billy's hole again and again. He heard Billy groaning, which he hoped meant he was doing well.

"God damn! You really gonna take that monster?" Billy asked.

"Just watch," Sean said, moving so that he was squatting over Jay's long dick.

Jay felt Sean grab his dick, and then the warmth of Sean's ass as it began to press against the tip of his cock. He trembled even more now. It was difficult to breathe with Billy's ass pressed firmly down on his face, but it was exciting, too. Jay pushed his tongue firmly against Billy's pucker and felt it open around it. The musky taste wasn't nearly as bad as Jay had worried, and he was soon wriggling his tongue inside of Billy, shoving it as deeply into it as he could.

Billy wriggled on his face, groaning and complimenting

him. Jay's body trembled intensely, and his heart hammered inside of him. The pressure on his dick increased as Sean put more weight onto it. It was almost painful.

Jay could not believe this was happening. It was beyond what he had dreamed, and more than he had fantasized. He had imagined being with two guys before, but he had never imagined having someone sitting on his face with someone else sitting on his dick, all while he was handcuffed and being made to do what they wanted.

Jay felt a great pressure on the head of his dick, so much that he wondered if Sean was going to open up enough to let him in or not. He began to wonder what would happen if he couldn't.

Billy seemed to notice too, and asked Sean if he was going to be man enough to take it or not.

"I will," Sean said firmly, and let more of his weight rest on the tip of Jay's cock. "Oh, fuck! I will!"

Jay began to whimper at the pain as his hard cock pressed against Billy's asshole. He tried again to free his hands, but he didn't know why, as he knew that there was no use.

"Just concentrate on my hole," Billy said.

Someone began twisting one of his nipples. Not very roughly, but enough to act as a warning. Jay redoubled his tongue's efforts against Billy's hole.

"That's the good boy," Billy cooed, squirming.

"Oh, shit!" Sean hissed.

Billy let most of his weight rest on Jay's face. Jay was finding it hard to breathe, but he liked what he was doing now. He would have been angry if Billy moved off of him now.

Jay felt Sean's hole opening around his head, finally. The hot hole spread open and Jay's cock began entering. Jay gasped as Billy's hole tightly slid down past the sensitive edges of his big head. Then the tight circle of Sean's ass began sliding down Jay's cock. It felt warm, silky, smooth, and tight. Jay shivered heavily all over and grunted into Billy's ass.

He licked Billy's hole with gusto, pushing his tongue into it and swirling it around the outside. He began to love it, began to enjoy it as much as he had ever enjoyed anything before. Between Billy sitting on his face and Sean sitting on his cock, Jay felt wonderful.

"Half!" Billy said gleefully. "Gonna make it?"

"Oh, hell yeah!" Sean said enthusiastically as he slid further down Jay's pole.

Sean grunted with the effort. Jay too. Billy growled deep inside as he wriggled on Jay's tongue. Jay couldn't see that Sean and Billy were kissing and jacking each other off, but he could hear the sounds of hands stroking slick, greased cocks. Even if he could have seen, he was too far into what he was doing to notice, anyway.

Jay let time fly past as he ate Billy's pink hole and Sean's ass finally came to rest on his hips. Jay heard them groaning, and he felt Billy's hole repeatedly spasm around his tongue. Billy grunted, and Jay felt the soft skin around his tongue and chin moving oddly, pulsating, then something warm and wet hit his belly. He knew what it was almost instantly, and before the second shot landed.

"Holy shit," Billy groaned.

Jay didn't relent as Billy came, instead, he worked his hole even harder with his tongue. It was incredible to Jay, feeling Billy's orgasm through his asshole with his tongue. Billy groaned, wriggled on Jay's face even more, and shuddered.

"Oh, damn! Yes! That's the shit!" Billy crooned.

"Oh, tell me!" Sean groaned. "Oh, man, gettin' close!"

Jay heard the sounds of Billy stroking Sean off, the Vaseline making a noise that Jay was familiar with on his own.

"Yeah, show me that cum!" Billy said smoothly. "Show me that wad! Cum like the pro you are!"

"Oh, shit! Keep jackin' like that! Like I like! Oh, fuck!"

Jay felt Sean's hole tighten on his cock and knew Sean was close to finishing. The waves of pleasure rolling through him were so intense that he was near to cumming himself.

"Yes!" Sean cried, and Jay felt the pucker tighten on his cock in waves, the timing matching the timing of the plops of warm fluid onto his chest.

"Nice!" Billy said. "Good one, man!"

"Oh, fuck!" Sean repeated several times.

Jay panted into Billy's ass, still licking and probing. He was proud of himself for not cumming, but he knew he wasn't going to last much longer at all. The waves of pleasure were meeting up between his legs and behind his balls, and he knew that soon he would be filling Sean's ass with his own waves of release.

Sean's orgasm wound down to its end, his hole still tightly gripping Jay's cock. Sean rested for a few moments, and Jay could hear them kissing and groaning together. He wanted in on it, badly.

Sean began rising, leaving Jay's cock. Jay wasn't far from cumming now, and wasn't sure if Sean was going to get off of him first, or if he was going to get off first. Jay's long cock popped out of Sean's ass and dropped to lay against his belly with a slap.

Billy and Sean climbed off of him and looked down at him with satisfied grins. Jay grinned back, waiting for his turn. The vision of the two of them, arm-in-arm, nearly over him, made Jay's cock pulse and push more pre-cum out and into his navel.

Billy's dick hung limp, shiny with Vaseline and cum. The patch of red hair was bright against his pale skin. His balls hung low, covered with red fuzz. His muscular frame was more rugged and stronger than Sean's, and much more so than Jay preferred.

The smaller, leaner Sean was more attractive to Jay. His longer, thicker cock was also hanging, shiny with Vaseline and his cum. His larger balls hung lower, too.

The two still breathed a little quickly as they stood arm-in-arm, looking down at Jay.

He wondered what they would do to finish him. He wanted Sean to sit on his cock again and ride him until he blasted his hot wad deep into his ass. If not that, he wanted to be blown off. He would accept a hand-job, anything. He just needed off. And soon.

"How long do we have?" Billy asked as he picked up the red ball with its strap.

"As long as you want. He doesn't have a class tomorrow until after noon."

"Cool," Billy said, his grin turning a little sadistic as he replaced the ball and fastened the strap. "Let's go grab some sliders and cool off before round two."

Sean put the hood over Jay's head again, and he knew he wasn't going to get off soon. He began to wonder if he was going to be gotten off at all.

Chapter 3

Jay could only lay there as Billy and Sean dressed and then left him alone, still handcuffed wrists and ankles to the bed, still gagged, still hooded, and their cum cooling on his belly and chest. His erection was throbbing now, and that only added to his frustration. He pulled on the cuffs, knowing that it was useless.

He was torn again. The need to reach orgasm warred with his desire to be free. He liked the sense of danger and uncertainty that he was in, but he was also worried that it was more than he could handle. He also liked the feeling as his balls ached to explode.

He wondered how long it would be before Billy and Sean would come back and release him – one way or another.

It seemed to be over an hour since they'd left, and he began worrying that maybe they were going to leave him there to be discovered by someone. That fear was almost intolerable, and he struggled to get free. He began to sweat and shiver, but now in worry and fear.

His breathing increased, and his heart began to hammer in his chest. He pulled on the cuffs, hurting his wrists and ankles with the effort. Worse, now he had to use the bathroom. Sean's and Billy's cum cooled and trickled down his sides, and that sensation was causing his bladder to insist on being emptied. Even worse, he could feel his bowels working as well.

Being unable to move made the need to urinate worsen. He began to rock his legs side to side in the effort not to piss on himself. He held it as long as he could, but urine was beginning to drip from him.

"Are we having a problem?" Sean asked from the door.

Jay nodded vigorously.

"Need out?"

Jay nodded again, even more enthusiastically.

Sean smiled as he sat on the edge of the bed. He ran his fingers up and down Jay's chest and belly, through the now cold cum. Jay's expression was frantic, and Sean noticed.

"Gotta use the john?"

Jay nodded violently.

Billy released the cuffs from the bed by undoing the black rubber straps, but didn't unlock the cuffs from his wrists and ankles. Sean wrapped his bathrobe over his shoulders and led him to the door. Jay protested. Sean laughed, made sure the bathrobe was closed and tied, then removed the gag.

"What if someone sees me?" Jay asked, frantic.

Sean told him, "If anyone asks, you're being hazed. Don't sweat it," and opened the door.

Sean led him to the bathroom by the cuffs as Jay shuffled, his ankles still cuffed. It was luck that there was no one else in the hall or bathroom. Sean led him into a stall and opened the bathrobe, arranged it as Jay sat, then left him to do his business. Jay called out when he was done. Jay had found it embarrassing to do what he needed to do with Sean standing there, but it was even more embarrassing when Sean bent him over and cleaned him up.

He didn't just clean Jay's hole, he cleaned him from waist to thighs, front and back, and especially between and under. By the time he was done, Jay was hard again, and the robe didn't hide that fact.

He was led back to the room, and the bed, where they cuffed him to it again, this time on his front, and unable to watch what Sean and Billy were doing. Jay felt even more helpless and out of control. He shook all over, some out of worry.

He felt fingers trace down his back, from shoulders to buttocks, then hands were massaging his butt cheeks. Another pair of hands were tickling between his thighs, barely touching the back of his ball sack from time to time. It was excruciating and highly erotic, and Jay's erection was nearly crushed beneath his own weight, as it wasn't placed comfortably.

Jay wiggled his hips, trying to find a more comfortable place for his long, hard cock, but he couldn't do so. The movements were adding to the sexual thrill, and Jay began shivering in that good way again. Until he saw Dexter near his face, one hand slowly spreading Vaseline along it. At that point, the shivers were no longer only sexual.

"I think he's afraid of Dex," Billy said with laughter in his voice.

"He should be, huh?" Sean replied.

"Oh, hell yeah!" Billy answered enthusiastically.

Jay silently agreed. His eyes followed the large dildo until it was taken out of his view behind him. He stretched his neck and craned his head to watch it as it neared his butt.

Sean moved so that he sat on his knees in front of Jay and pulled his head around, removed the ball, then stuffed his large dick into Jay's mouth.

"Dude, pay attention to my meat, or Billy is gonna shove Dex in, no getting you ready first. Get me?"

Jay responded by licking and sucking Sean's dick as well as he could. He tried to remember what Sean had liked before and concentrated on repeating them. The threat of having the enormous dildo shoved into his unready ass was thrilling, and Jay found it very satisfying. He was sure they would if he didn't at least suck and lick Sean as well as he had before, but he was almost sure that they wouldn't hurt him, either. That uncertainty added even more to his thrills as Billy's fingers probed and traced around his hole.

Sean moved so that his thighs were under Jay's restrained arms, took a handful of Jay's hair, then shoved the entire length of his cock into Jay's mouth and into his throat. Just as yesterday, Jay choked once the bulbous head passed into his throat. This time Sean relented, pulling enough of his dick out of Jay's mouth so that Jay could breathe again, then began fucking his mouth vigorously, now with two handfuls of his hair.

Jay applied all the suction he could and kept his tongue moving. He loved the feeling of a cock in his mouth. Having Sean's long, thick cock in his mouth was a long-time dream and fantasy come true. For the second day in a row, Jay let himself fall into a trance, only the cock in his mouth and his own movements and actions registering on his mind. Jay let the smell and taste of Sean fill his senses again, and a tense, powerful thrill filled him.

"Damn! He's gonna suck the skin off it!" Sean groaned.

"Man, his face full of your cock is so hot!" Billy crooned from next to Jay's face.

Jay didn't open his eyes and hardly heard Billy at all. He was filled with the taste, smell, and sensations of Sean's cock on his tongue and in his mouth. The desire to use his hands to touch and feel Sean's cock, his balls, the rest of his body, was intense. Jay tried to get his hands free, but not consciously – it was mere instinct and desire. The cuffs didn't give an inch, and the struggle was useless.

Jay's mind forgot about the handcuffs when he felt fingers spreading the cheeks of his ass. At Sean's urging, Billy applied Vaseline to Jay's hole with a finger, then began sliding that finger in and out of Jay. Sean ordered Billy not to touch Jay's sweet spot.

The first taste of pre-cum caused a low, deep groan from Jay. The way Sean's cock swelled and pulsed as the pre-cum was pushed through it made Jay feel weak all through his body. When the salty taste flowed over his tongue, Jay shuddered and was unable to stop the guttural groan.

"Oh, he likes that," Billy crooned. "He's a natural cock sucker."

"Damned right he is," Sean agreed. "Not a single lesson, but he's doing great!"

"He's never, before? With anyone?"

"Have you?" Sean asked after pulling his long cock free of Jay's mouth.

Jay shook his head, his smile obvious. Sean shoved his cock against Jay's lips and then through them. Jay went happily back to work on it. Without Sean shoving it into his mouth, Jay bobbed on the top half of it, paying a lot of attention to the edges of the bulbous head with his tongue.

"Oh, fuck me! He's fucking awesome!"

Sean arched his back and shoved himself forward, groaning as Jay worked on his cock with suction, tongue, and lips.

Jay felt Billy inserting something larger than his own finger into him, but too small to be his penis. He wasn't sure what it was, but Jay liked how it felt, and even lifted his ass toward it, wanting more of the sensation.

Billy was grinning widely as he watched his thick finger disappear and reappear through Jay's tight, tan hole. His other hand cupped Jay's balls and played with them after tugging them back and down between Jay's thighs. They were larger than his own and Sean's, and Billy couldn't keep himself from playing with them. He shoved both fingers into Jay's ass as deeply as he could, then flattened his hand against Jay's butt cheek so that he could get his face between Jay's thighs and his balls into his mouth.

Jay groaned around Sean's cock when he felt the warm, wet sensation on his sack. He wasn't sure what it was, but he liked it a lot. As his balls were bathed in the warmth, and Billy's tongue worked on them, Jay groaned nearly continually and had to force himself not to writhe around and make it harder for Billy to do whatever he was doing to him.

Jay was sure he was going to cum, and was looking forward to it. Billy stopped far too soon, though. The delicious pressure had been building up down there, finally, and Jay wanted that release badly. Now that Billy had stopped, Jay felt as if his balls were swelling, almost painfully.

If he didn't have his mouth full of Sean's long cock, Jay would have begged Billy to go back to work on him. Instead, Jay almost squirmed when he felt two fingers slide into him.

"He's pretty tight, Sean. I think we'll have to teach him how to make it easier," Billy said.

"You listen to Bill, and do what he says, or since he's in the perfect position, he'll have to spank you," Sean said, holding Jay's head so that they could see each other eye to eye.

Jay nodded, not slowing on Sean's dick one beat. Sean smiled and nodded at him, then nodded at Billy.

Billy began giving Jay instructions on how to loosen himself. Jay followed them, and soon Billy was moving three of his thick fingers in and out of Jay's hole.

"Gettin' there," Billy said happily, then added another finger.

Jay groaned deeply around the near agony as the four thick fingers slid into him. He did as Billy had instructed him, and the fingers slid in without any further pain.

"Nice," Billy crooned. "Good job. You're gonna be one hot ass."

Jay wriggled gently as Billy shoved his fingers into him again and again, and as Sean's cock fucked his mouth, more and more forcefully. Jay was sure Sean was nearing his orgasm now, as Sean moved faster and with more energy. Sean also started groaning softly, and his head was thrown back. Sean tightened his grip on Jay's hair with both hands and pulled his face further down his long, thick cock. Jay gagged a bit as the thick head entered his throat, and Sean stayed there.

Jay swallowed nervously. The sensation made Sean whimper and shiver. Jay noticed and swallowed again. Sean groaned an, "Oh, God!"

Jay loved it. He was giving Sean so much pleasure, and Jay found he loved knowing that. Jay could feel Sean's entire body shivering now, and he could hear Sean's breath coming rapidly and roughly. When Sean groaned, "Oh, fuck, I'm going off!" Jay stretched out his neck so that he could take in even more of Sean's very long cock, and sucked as hard as he could. His tongue lashed the underside of it.

Sean squealed and locked rigidly in place with his back arched and the fingers of both hands wrapped in Jay's curly, sandy hair. Sean's cock began throbbing and twisting. Sean's balls moved upward and nearly disappeared.

Sean hissed, "Oh, fuck!" in a high voice, then crumpled over Jay's head as his orgasm raced through his body. His breath stopped, and only short, sharp gasps escaped as he fired his cum into Jay's mouth. Each orgasmic expulsion was paired with a strong twitch of his cock, a small shove of his hips, and a small, quiet, high-pitched, "Oh!"

Jay was in bliss as he felt Sean's cock dance in his mouth. Each thick, hot, slimy, sticky, gooey, salty, musky expulsion of semen filled his mouth to nearly overflowing. He swallowed happily each time, ready for the next. Seven distinct shots and seven deep swallows later, Sean fell onto Jay's back with a gasp.

Jay didn't stop licking and sucking, and Sean's entire body began to shiver and twitch with the pleasure. Sean's cock was thrashing wildly under Jay's attentions, and he could barely contain the intense pleasure Jay's mouth was giving him.

"Give it to him," Sean was barely able to say past his panting breath.

Sean leaned over Jay's back, pulled apart Jay's ass cheeks, and massaged them powerfully as Jay felt Billy moving around between his legs. Jay wanted to look over his shoulder and behind him, to see what Billy was going to do, but Sean's cock was still in his mouth and his body draped over his head and back.

Jay felt Billy applying more cold Vaseline to his opening. It wasn't long before Jay knew what 'it' Billy was going to give him. His mind rapidly replayed all the tips and instructions Billy had taught him just a few minutes ago. He pushed and relaxed himself, preparing for the painful entry of Dexter.

"Hang on, lemme get it ready," Sean said.

Billy moved, and Jay was sure that he was now sitting on his butt. He heard the familiar sounds of sucking. Very soon Billy began moaning. Jay was sure he could feel Billy's balls laying along the top of his butt crack. That excited him. When he felt Billy sliding forward and back, and his balls sliding along his crack, Jay felt himself climbing toward release. He moaned around Sean's thick cock still in his mouth. It had softened, but was still large and felt heavy. That it was soft didn't lessen how much Jay enjoyed having it in his mouth. His tongue still roamed over its surfaces, and it responded with a twitch now and then, Sean letting out a soft moan or gasp.

Jay wasn't sure how close he could get to cumming without actually doing it, but he knew he was close to finishing as he had ever been without actually shooting. His cock felt as if it were pumped up beyond normal fullness. The pressure inside of it was almost painful. Each heartbeat threatened to rupture it like a balloon. If Billy weren't sitting on his buttocks, making it impossible to do so, Jay would have humped his hips against the bed and surely soaked the sheet with his wad. He almost cried out with the need to cum.

For long minutes Jay lay there, on the very edge of orgasm, as Sean sucked Billy's dick and Billy's balls slid teasingly along the crack of Jay's ass. The taste and aroma of Sean's cum was gone now, and Jay wanted more of it. He continued to lick and suck on Sean's cock, which began to harden and lengthen again. Sean shivered from time to time, but kept sucking on Billy's dick until Billy warned him.

"If you keep goin', man, I'm gonna blast!"

Billy moved, and soon Jay felt something against his hole. It was warm and solid, and Jay wasn't so sure it was Dexter. As it pushed against his hole, he felt Billy's legs against his own, and was now sure it was Billy that was about to enter him.

Billy's cock was shorter but thicker than Sean's. Jay had taken Sean's long, thick cock yesterday, so Jay's fears of pain receded but remained. It was painful as Billy's thick cock pushed against his hole and began to enter him. Jay remembered the lessons and did what he could to make it easier.

As Billy's head pushed into him, Jay almost came. The pressure and pain raised his state of sexual tension even higher. As Billy's cock slid deeper into him, Jay tensed in extreme pleasure. Between the long, thick cock in his mouth and the fat cock entering his ass, Jay felt a thrill he had never before.

Billy's every movement sent thrills through Jay. Powerful shivers ran through his body along with what felt like electrical sparks all along his nerves.

Sean began thrusting in and out of his mouth again, seemingly in time with Billy's thrusts in and out of his ass. The movements of the two boys made Jay feel as if he were being pulled apart and then crushed back together between them. His breathing had no choice but to match the timing of the two boys as they filled and emptied him again and again.

Long, long minutes passed as Billy fucked his ass and Sean fucked his mouth. Jay could hear them kissing behind and above him. Their moans and groans were timed between kisses and gasps for breath. Jay was lost in the sensations that ruled his body and mind. The pressure in his groin began moving outward, into his gut and back. It almost felt as if his body were expanding from a central point between his balls and hole, the skin covering the rest of his body having to stretch to accommodate his growing size. Every muscle in his body seemed to be shivering as they struggled to contain the extreme pleasure.

"Sean, oh, man, gonna!"

"Fill him up!"

"Oh, fuck!"

Jay felt Billy's cock thrust deep into him, deeper than before, and hold there, quivering, throbbing, pulsating. It hurt at first, but almost instantly turned into a deep, heavy, warm pleasure. Jay could feel Billy's pubes against the cheeks of his ass, and his balls between his thighs. He was sure he could feel warm fluid filling his bowels as Billy groaned wordlessly and shivered against him.

"Oh, God! Oh, God!" Billy panted again and again.

Jay could feel the heat of Billy's body against his ass and back, the sweat on his skin, the trembling of his muscles. Billy slowly slumped until he rested his weight on Jay's back. He shivered as he panted and softly groaned in pleasure. Billy's rapid, heavy breath blew across the back of Jay's neck.

"Oh, shit. Jay, you got a great ass!" Billy groaned into Jay's ear.

"Climb off, I wanna tap that again before I blow," Sean said quickly.

Jay hated it when Sean removed his cock from his mouth. He wanted it to stay there forever. It was the most incredible experience of his life. He loved sucking cock, he'd learned that yesterday, but today he needed it.

Billy and Sean traded places quickly, and before he knew it, Jay was sucking a greasy, shitty cock. He didn't care. It was his own ass he tasted, beside the flavor of Billy's cum and the Vaseline. He sucked and licked the fat cock just as ardently as he had Sean's. Billy shoved all five or six thick inches into Jay's mouth. Jay could take every bit of it, though it was much thicker than Sean's much longer one.

He felt Sean sitting on his thighs, and he knew he was smearing Vaseline on himself. Jay's hole twitched and tingled, ready and wanting more, but knowing what was coming was longer.

The sensation of the cold Vaseline covering the tip of Sean's cock made Jay's hole slam shut. He didn't want it to, and had to concentrate to relax it. His mind was losing the battle as Sean began pushing against his hole. It remained clenched, and Jay had to concentrate solely on his sphincter, ignoring the cock in his mouth.

Sean pushed, and Jay winced. In that movement, he took control and willed the muscles to loosen. As Sean pushed further, the pain and tension increased. Jay willed those muscles to relax with all his thoughts. Sean pushed and his head spread Jay open and slid into him.

Sean grunted as his head vanished, and Jay shivered beneath his hands. Jay's little whimpers were lost around

Billy's cock. Billy was being patient, knowing and feeling how much Sean was doing to him. Billy waited as Jay struggled to take Sean, slowly and gently sliding his dick in and out of Jay's nearly open mouth.

Sean moved on the bed, closing the distance between his dark pubes and Jay's white ass cheeks. His long dick slid further into Jay, nearly half of it now between the slim cheeks. Sean slowly lowered his body, pushing more of himself inside of Jay. Jay shivered strongly below him, the light sweat from Billy's fucking now heavier and covering all of Jay's tall, slim, white body.

Sean came to rest on Jay's buttocks with a sigh. With a long sigh of his own, Jay relaxed.

"Oh, yes!" Sean crooned. "I can feel your cum inside him!"

Sean remained motionless, enjoying the warm silky insides wrapped tightly around his sensitive head. Jay shivered violently, then began working enthusiastically on Billy with his mouth.

Billy sighed deeply as Jay's lips closed around him, his tongue began moving over him, and the suction began. Billy moved his hips gently as Jay bobbed up and down on him.

Jay felt his body burning. The sensation of Sean's cock deep in him again was intense. His desire to cum coupled with that was overwhelming. Added to that was the pleasure of a cock in his mouth. Jay felt like he never had before.

When Sean began making small, short movements, Jay ground his hips backward, onto him. Doing so moved his cock against the bed and caused waves of pleasure to race from the tip of his cock down deep into his groin. Waves of pleasure, as if he were cumming, tore through him. His cock danced and pounded against the bed, and his hole clamped down on Sean's cock. The pain caused by Sean's dick in his hole as the spasm occurred nearly caused Jay to cry out.

"No stopping!" Billy said loudly, then slapped Jay hard.

Jay jerked in surprise and at the pain. That caused his hole to clamp down on Sean's cock again, and the pain on his face and in his ass, and the other sensations together, did something new to Jay.

With a rush of hot pain in his ass, his cock jerked against the bed and began releasing an orgasm that had been held back for far too long. Again and again, Jay's hole clamped down on

Sean's cock as cum rushed up and through him. Jay couldn't have paid any attention to Billy's cock now if he had to. His entire body and mind were being crushed together and torn apart at the same time.

His body tensed, his hole clamped down, his muscles beneath his balls throbbed as something there sent waves of an intense, strange sensation through him, and his hot semen flowed onto the sheets. Again and again, and with each one, Jay groaned loudly from deep within. Pain and pleasure mixed, overwhelming Jay as he had never felt before. Each wave of cum through him felt as if it were on fire. He couldn't breathe, except between convulsions of his orgasm. Sean's cock was ripping his hole open with each one.

Jay didn't hear Sean saying, "Holy shit!" over and over. Nor did he hear Billy's words of admiration. Jay only convulsed around his groin, pulling the chains of the handcuffs taut each time. His body wanted to curl into a tight ball, but the cuffs wouldn't allow it. The hard, long cock in his ass felt like a steel bar. Billy's cock was still in his mouth, but he couldn't close his lips around it and still breathe.

After what felt like several minutes of endless, nearly unbearable pleasure, Jay's body relaxed. He was able to breathe again and did so by panting rapidly.

In only seconds, Sean began moving in and out of him again, and Billy shoved his dick all the way into his mouth. Jay knew what they expected, and he knew he had to give it. His body was still coming down from the incredible sensations of the most powerful orgasm of his life, and he wanted to relax, but he wasn't done so long as Billy and Sean weren't done, and he knew it.

Jay returned to sucking Billy's cock. Billy hardly moved, sitting on his knees and legs, letting Jay bob up and down on his short, fat cock. Sean began moving quickly, the sensation of his large cock moving in and out of him causing Jay to wriggle on it uncontrollably.

All three boys groaned and gasped quietly. It wasn't long before Sean was moving quickly and deeply enough to slap his skin against the skin of Jay's ass.

"Oh, fuck! He's so tight!"

"He sucks like a pro!"

"I'm gonna soon!"

"Me too!"

"Together?"

"Fuck yeah!"

Jay was being fucked hard enough now that his cock was being pushed against the bed again. Despite the incredible orgasm just minutes ago, Jay felt as if he were going to have another. He found a way to let his hips move even more and using Sean's movements to increase his own pleasure. He heard Sean and Billy giving each other cues, warning each other that they were going to cum. Jay knew he was going to as well, if only he could before Sean finished.

Jay moved his hips in odd ways, into unusual positions, and found one that caused Sean's cock to hit that special place more often. It was all Jay could do not to scream in pleasure each time Sean's cock hit it.

Billy warned Sean that he was going to finish very soon, and Sean began fucking Jay even harder. Sean asked Billy to slow down, and Billy responded by removing most of his cock from Jay's mouth.

Jay worked the smooth, rounded, almost pointed head of Billy's cock. Billy's six inches slid smoothly back into Jay's mouth just as Sean cried out.

Sean pushed deeply into Jay, crushing Jay's cock against the bed, pulling the skin of his penis further back than it was accustomed to. The slight pain was exquisite. He could feel Sean's cock pulsing and swelling as his hot cum flowed into him. Then, suddenly, Billy was pushing his cock all the way into Jay's mouth as it swelled and pulsed. The hot cum from Billy, the taste, feel, smell of it, sent Jay even further into a hazy, nearly absent state.

Jay was seconds from exploding again, but Sean pulled out of his ass and Billy from his mouth, and Jay was left trembling on the edge of release. Sean and Billy fell onto to bed beside him. The two of them panted and complimented Jay on his performance.

Jay trembled with unreleased pressure as he knew he had to wait. Again.

Chapter 4

Jay needed off. He began thrusting his hips, rubbing his erection against the bed.

Sean slapped his ass hard enough to sting, and said, "No!"

Jay whimpered, but also grinned. It was both pleasure and torture. His penis throbbed between his body and the bed, begging to finish. The pressure behind his scrotum pulsed, threatening to erupt, but it slowly subsided.

Sean's and Billy's fingers roamed all over his back, butt, and thighs. When they first found their way between his crack, he shivered.

One of them positioned himself between his spread thighs. Fingers applied Vaseline to his slightly sore hole, one finger at a time, ending with three of them after less than a minute. Jay was enjoying it, more than he had suspected that he would. The pain was minimal, but hot, too.

When the fingers rotated and pushed into the area behind his balls, Jay writhed on them. Heavy tingles exploded within the area, sending him into shivers and shudders. He'd had no idea that such sensations could be created. Intense, rapid vibrations seemed to swell outward from that point as the fingers massaged there. Jay bit down, refusing to make a noise. The chains of the cuffs rattled as Jay shuddered.

"Jeeze. I think you found his calling," Billy said, laughter in his voice.

"No kiddin', huh?" Sean replied, also sounding amused. "First time I hit yours, you went nuts, too."

"Not like that," Billy said firmly.

"Maybe," Sean replied. "I bet he'll finish!"

"Oh, no shit! Make him!"

"I bet he will," Sean said as he began massaging Jay's prostate more vigorously.

Jay convulsed in time with Sean's actions, unable to do anything else. He simply lost control of his body at the touch. The electrical waves of incredible pleasure were more than he could take. His cock throbbed with the motions, too, and what felt like the entire contents of his balls began coursing up through the same area.

Jay gagged on his own breath as his body went into spasms timed to Sean's movements on his prostate. His breath came in short gasps between those spasms. The pressure inside his groin grew to unbearable levels. His semen was forced through that bottleneck with a pressure he wasn't familiar with. It was as if all of his previous orgasms had only clogged his plumbing, and this one was finally scouring the path clear.

Every muscle drew taut, even his breathing stopped. Only Sean's fingers and that organ moved, but the movement created by that small organ caused further movement of his lengthy penis as the thick, heavy orgasm fired from his cock harder than he could remember it having done before.

He was unable to scream, not because of Sean's order, but because his entire body was locked and rigid. Jay thought he could hear the sound of his semen roaring through his cock. The orgasm was deep and strong, but slow and almost steady. Instead of individual powerful squirts, it was nearly one constant wash of fluid, despite the pulsing of his organ as it pumped it through him.

It also seemed to go on forever. By the time his body suddenly returned to his control, he was sweating and his sight was narrowed and blurred. His breath came back in deep, rapid, ragged gasps. He wasn't sure if the fingers were still in him or not, or if he had gone numb. Shrinking waves of pleasure washed down through him.

"Too bad it got wasted in the bed," Sean said sadly.

"No shit. Bet that was a nice, big one."

Jay nodded, then shivered violently. When he was able to think again, he felt movement on the bed and saw Sean's erection approaching his face. He barely had time to open his mouth before the hot shaft thrust into it.

Jay moved like a cat and took the long shaft. He gulped and moaned as he took nearly all of Sean's length. That earned him a sharp slap on his ass from Billy. He winced, but never lost track of his tongue on Sean's cock. He needed it. He wanted it more than he wanted anything.

"Oh, God! He sucks so fucking good!" Sean crooned.

Sean groaned and pumped his cock in and out of Jay's mouth. With another growling groan, Sean slunk even lower and threw his head back, his body arching from his hips.

Jay locked his lips over the middle of Sean's long cock and sucked. His tongue slowly undulated along the underside of it. He moved his head as much as his neck allowed. He craned his neck and forced more into his mouth. He felt the large head on the back of his throat and wanted more. He forced more in, but the gagging got in the way. He couldn't take the entire length of it. He bobbed, moving down as far as he could every time, trying to take more and more of it.

"Fucking hell! It's like he's sucking it right out! Fuck!"

Sean grabbed two hands full of Jay's hair and held on. His hips pumped his long cock through Jay's lips. Sean gasped and groaned. Both of his balls crept upward and his sack tightened up around them. They nearly vanished, and Sean became shiny with sweat.

Jay was lost. All that existed was his mouth and Sean's cock, and that's all that needed to exist. It was all that Jay ever needed. He would do anything for it. He would do anything its owner told him to do.

He wriggled forward the best he could and shoved his head downward, taking Sean's cock all the way down his throat. He needed to swallow to do it, but he took it all, until his nose was pressed into Sean's dark-brown bush.

"Oh, God!" Sean repeated several times. "Fucking hell! That's amazing!"

Sean couldn't keep quiet. He groaned, moaned, cried out expletives, complimented Jay, or told Billy how good Jay was doing, at all times. It wasn't all that long a period of time, either, but Sean looked as if he had just finished an overtime game. He panted rapidly between words.

Jay took the entire length of Sean's cock again and again. The need to gag when it entered his throat was ignored now, and the sensation of wrapping his throat around Sean's cock was pure bliss. The feeling of it twitching and pulsating in his throat was even more intimate than in his ass. Jay was lost. Or found.

Jay slid the entire way down Sean again, and Sean bucked, then cried out, "Awww, FUCK!"

Jay heard Sean's cry and felt his body shudder through his cock. He knew what was happening. The salty nectar came again, this time with a hint of musk, and he yearned for it. He slid down as far as he could onto Sean's long cock, his gag reflex now merely an annoyance he could ignore.

Then Sean was quiet. He arched forward over Jay's head and held on tightly as his entire body convulsed repeatedly. His broken breaths were the only sounds for long seconds. Sean jerked several times, silently, only gasps of breath between them.

"Awwwwww, fuuuuck," and then Sean lay back and panted, protecting his sore cock from Jay's attempts to reclaim it.

"He needs more, Billy. Get over here and take care of it."

Sean moved away, and Billy took his place. Jay inhaled Billy, and in mere seconds Billy was bucking and pumping, crying out and complimenting Jay.

Billy's cock didn't even enter Jay's throat once he slid down him and nearly remained there entirely, his nose buried in Billy's short, red bush. His tongue moved over and around Billy's cock, sending Billy into fits and starts.

"Oh, damn! He can suck!" Billy exclaimed, grinning widely.

Billy wound into wordless expressions of adulation for Jay's abilities. He pumped his hips as fast and wildly as he liked. At first, his balls swung and slapped Jay's chin, but soon they were tucked up high and tight in the pink sack. Billy ended up in the same position as Sean had been when he finished. Billy even ended nearly as silently, curved over Jay's head, cock buried to the hilt in his mouth.

Once Billy collapsed, Jay lay there and panted, overjoyed. He didn't care if he came again or not. He had felt fulfilled after the earlier orgasm, the oral fun with Sean and then Billy had just been icing on the cake. What Sean had done to him from inside his ass had left him feeling as if he couldn't come again for days.

He wasn't even sure if he was hard or not. And he didn't think he really cared. He was happy.

The ball-gag was placed firmly in his mouth again, and the hood was placed over his head again. Jay was worn out. The sweat was drying on his body, and he wanted nothing more than to shower and sleep. He was startled when someone reached under him and groped for his cock.

"He's hard," Sean said, a grin in his voice.

"After that wad he blew into the bed? I'd be soft for hours!"

"Even after sucking off two dicks?"

"Oh, yeah. Guess that'd get it back up, huh?"

"Did him! Come hold his hips up while I put Victoria on him."

Billy held Jay's hips up while Sean slid something beneath him. Jay couldn't tell what it was.

"Now, Jay, all you gotta do is fuck Victoria until you finish. If you don't finish, we don't take off the cuffs, and leave you like that all night."

Sean's voice was firm, but it held a little humor, too. Jay was almost sure they wouldn't leave him there like that, but he wasn't all that sure.

Billy released his hips and Jay felt a smooth, soft, delicious feeling as his cock slid into something. His body tensed and shivered as the skin on his cock was pushed backward as it slid further into whatever it was.

Experimentally, he slowly raised his hips, the sensation on his cock thrilling him deeply. He thrust forward, bringing his hips back down, and grunted behind the ball-gag as his cock slid back into the soft, smooth place that gripped it so wonderfully.

"That's it, Jay, just enjoy it. When I get back from the shower, I want to see you either going to town, or all done, and a nice big load inside her. One or the other."

"I'll make sure he keeps going," Billy said enthusiastically, then softly slapped Jay's butt cheeks.

With a soft groan, Jay began thrusting his hips up and down, sliding his long dick through the mysterious Victoria. It felt like he imagined a vagina would. It was tight enough that the skin over his hard core was moved firmly front to back, yet yielding enough that it felt soft on it.

Several times he pushed as far into it as he could and found there was room enough for his entire length. With his arms cuffed over his head and his ankles still cuffed, it was a little uncomfortable and awkward, but it felt so good.

Jay began to sweat again. He thrust again and again, varying as his muscles and his cock complained in fatigue. Billy's hands roamed over his butt, between his thighs, and around his hips. Jay's breath quickened again, and tremors began in his tired, weakened muscles.

Jay heard Sean come back from his shower and tell Billy to take his turn. Jay knew that the hands now roaming over his back, ass, and thighs were Sean's. When Jay felt his balls cupped and fondled, he knew who it was. And when a tongue found its way between his cheeks and into his ass, he knew who's it was.

That tongue drove Jay insane. The sensations in his cock as it slid through Victoria were new and wonderful, and nearly overloaded Jay's senses again, but the addition of Sean's tongue on, around, and inside of his hole drove him further.

With waves of powerful sensations coursing through his body like never before, his tired, aching prostate performed yet again. As the convulsions began between his balls and his hole, the tongue vanished and was replaced by strong, solid, probing fingers that found the sensitive spot without fail and began massaging it.

With a scream, even behind the red ball, Jay's body convulsed powerfully. The chains of the handcuffs rattled as Jay thrashed and bucked. Each orgasmic spasm closed his aching hole around Sean's fingers, nearly painfully, and so incredibly pleasurably.

"Holy fuck, Sean!" Billy said gleefully.

"He's having the time of his life," Sean said, his fingers stabbing and stroking Jay's insides.

Over and over, Jay's body convulsed, tugging the chains tight each time.

"Damn!" Billy said, sitting on the bed and reaching out and under Sean's hand to cup Jay's balls and play with them, trying to follow the sudden, sharp movements of Jay's body as it released wave after wave of semen. "I think he's gonna pump dry!"

"No shit!" Sean agreed gleefully.

The both of them continued working Jay's body as his balls emptied into Victoria. Even after Jay's orgasm ended, his body jerked as spasms rang through it like shadows of his orgasm. For long minutes Billy and Sean played with Jay's sweating, heaving, shivering body.

Jay's breath was ragged and quick, snot and sweat soaking his upper lip and the red ball strapped into his mouth. Jay's curly blond hair was plastered to his forehead and around his ears.

Billy removed the hood and the ball-gag. Jay's eyes could barely focus, the lids barely fluttering open on rare occasions.

"I think you broke him," Billy said with a giggle.

"He'll heal. Might take a while," Sean said with a giggle as well.

Jay felt as if he'd run a marathon, then swam across a lake, and then biked over a mountain pass. Every muscle was tired, and many were sore. His penis felt as if it had been run over by a truck. And the ache in his anus threatened to be with him for a while.

But he felt fantastic! Satisfied like never before. He understood the word 'satiated' for the first time.

Sean's hand slid over the hot, smooth skin of Jay's ass. He fondled and caressed the cheeks. Jay wanted to moan, but he hadn't been given permission, so he held it back. His breathing increased, and he was surprised to feel his penis growing erect again. He began lifting and dropping his hips, sliding his slick penis in and out of the object again.

"Holy shit! You humping Victoria again?" Sean asked.

Jay snickered and stopped.

Sean laughed, then said, "I didn't think you'd be able to! Not right now, anyway. Especially after earlier."

Billy slid one of his blunt fingers into Jay's ass and began massaging his prostate again. Jay whimpered, and received a slap to the back of his head. His cock was almost sore, and moving it through the fake vagina was slightly painful, but it was far more pleasurable than painful. In moments, Jay's body was filled with sexual energy and his skin and muscles were tingling again.

Sean moved his hand up and down Jay's buttocks and back, giving Jay intense thrills. Jay began fucking the fake vagina with gusto, making the bed squeak.

"Not too fast or loud," Sean warned.

That, too, increased Jay's thrill. The strike hadn't come, but he knew it could, and that raised the stakes, which made Jay feel almost high. He panted now as he fucked Victoria, as Sean's hand roamed over his buttocks, and Billy's finger rubbed his insides. Jay shuddered and gasped as his cock released a wave of pre-cum.

Sean continued stroking the soft, tender skin between Jay's thighs, running over his buttocks, and caressing his thighs and lower back. Billy added a second thick finger in his ass and on his prostate. Jay was shivering all over, new sweat breaking out all over his body.

Jay bit into the blanket and held back the cry of near pain and pleasure as Billy pushed a third thick finger into him. Jay pushed his hips up and his legs apart, inviting the digits as deeply as possible without leaving the fake vagina. Only after holding there a few moments did he thrust his hips forward, shoving his long cock deeply into Victoria.

Billy's expert fingers worked the sensitive spot inside of him, and then were joined by his thumb on the outside, and Jay groaned deep in his chest. Suddenly his body went into overdrive and tensed tightly. He was unable to move as an urgent, powerful orgasm took over his body.

His prostate pulsed, his cock pulsed, his body tensed. Again and again. Jay struggled not to cry out as each powerful ejaculation released more cum into the tight, wet grasp of the fake vagina. The new, warm fluid changed the feel of the device on Jay's cock, which intensified the sensation and added more to Jay's orgasm.

Billy's fingers inside of him and his thumb outside worked Jay's prostate as his orgasm screamed through him. Billy pushed and released in time with Jay's orgasm, Jay's long cock bottoming out in the soft, warm, wet, fake vagina.

Jay groaned, "Fuck!" softly but firmly through the gag.

Billy laughed softly as he felt the mechanics of Jay's orgasm with his thumb and fingers. He was fascinated by the sensations of Jay's anus and prostate as Jay's orgasm occurred.

When Jay's body tensed even tighter and held that tension even longer, Billy knew Jay's orgasm was ending and he slowly removed his fingers.

The last few convulsions of Jay's hole, now without Billy's fingers in it, intensified the last waves of his orgasm. Jay cried out softly, holding back as much as he could.

The weird sensation of the fluids squelching around the head of his cock inside the tight, slick embrace of the fake vagina was another entirely new sensation that Jay loved.

Shivers and shudders ran through him, powerful and persistent. They seemed to take complete control for long seconds, even his breathing now ragged and irregular.

Finally, his body relaxed and he exhaled loudly, shivers still running through him. The squelching sensation as his long cock compacted his semen inside of Victoria made him shiver.

"You can really go to town! That's what? Three?" Sean asked as he removed the gag.

"I won't be able to again forever!" Jay laughed.

"Shhh!" Sean reminded him again.

"Shit," Jay replied, softly.

Billy removed the cuffs from his ankles, and Sean took off the cuffs on his wrists. Jay rubbed his wrists as he rolled over. His cock slid out of the fake vagina, making him shudder powerfully. His muscles complained at nearly every movement, causing him to groan and moan more, but differently now.

He noticed that the room smelled like sex and sweat. Then he noticed that his bed looked like a murder scene, but some colorless fluid instead of blood soaking his sheets.

Sean picked up the vinyl, tube-shaped object and carefully placed it into his overnight bag, saying, "You about split Victoria open! I never seen so much cum in it before!"

The large wet spot on his blanket was obvious. So were the sweat stains where he had lain so long.

"Better do laundry tomorrow. Going to need clean sheets again," Sean said commandingly.

"Oh, gawd," Jay groaned, smiling.

"Not tomorrow, Sean. Practice all day, remember? He'll have to beat the meat alone tomorrow," Billy said.

"No, he won't. He won't get hard again for days," Jay moaned into his hands, both saddened and relieved he would have tomorrow off.

His tone caused both Sean and Billy to laugh.

Over the next few minutes, Billy and Sean helped Jay to flip the mattress and put clean sheets on the bed.

"How ya fellin'?" Sean asked once the bed was arranged.

"Like you do after soccer practice, I guess" Jay replied with a half-grin.

"That worn out, huh? Well, you better clean your plate and take your vitamins, 'cause next time I'm gonna test your endurance."

Jay quailed at that prospect. He was exhausted right then, and if that wasn't what Sean called testing his endurance, he wasn't sure he wanted his endurance tested.

"Wish we didn't have practice all day and shit tomorrow. You're fuckin' fun, Jay," Billy said a little sadly.

Jay laughed a bit nervously and blushed darkly. He wasn't used to being talked to so nicely by others, let alone being complimented. Having a new friend, or at least a friend of a new friend, talk to him that way was new, and felt wonderful.

"No jerking it tomorrow, Jay. Save it," Sean commanded.

Jay grimaced, but he knew he would obey. He wanted to obey.

"We have to figure out when we can do stuff over the weekend," Sean said.

"We have practice Saturday for most of the day, but that night is free," Billy said.

"Oh, my God!" Jay suddenly snapped loudly.

"What the hell?" Sean and Billy asked at the same time.

"My parents' cabin! They won't be there this weekend!"

Three huge grins lit up the room.

Chapter 5

It had been so long! Only two days, but it had seemed a week, at least.

The wait Friday night, while Billy and Sean had been at practice, had seemed to last forever. When they'd arrived, they were too exhausted for sex and commanded Jay to refrain from masturbation yet again. He'd obeyed.

Saturday had been horrible. All morning and afternoon alone, and he wasn't allowed to masturbate again. Sean had commanded him not to relieve himself, not to even touch himself. While that had been easy to agree to on Thursday, and he'd managed to refrain on Friday, it had become difficult Saturday. Jay seemed to get hard automatically and without a single sexual thought. And it stayed hard for much longer than normal.

But he'd managed. He had stayed busy by doing schoolwork, watching television, and playing video games. He'd showered, paced, and dozed off. It was a knock on the door that woke him.

He dashed to the door, excited and grinning from ear to ear, expecting Billy. He flung open the door, smiling, and said, "Hey!"

His smile left instantly as he took in the short, black, straight hair, the black eyes, the round face and narrow lips, wide shoulders and strong arms of Paul Rogers.

"Jay, how's stuff?" Paul asked, smiling in return.

"Paul! Uh, so, what's up?" Jay asked.

Paul had been one of his very few friends in high school. Senior year, they'd hardly spoken. He had liked Paul, quite a bit, and had worried that his attraction to Paul would one day be figured out by him or someone else. He had stopped hanging out with him very often, suspecting that Paul was beginning to figure him out. When Pauls stopped trying to hang out with him, he'd been both relieved and let down about losing Paul's friendship. But he was mostly glad that he wouldn't have to face him. So it was almost shocking to see Paul at his dorm.

"Nothing, really. Just, I thought, what the hell, go see what Jay's up to, ya know?"

Paul shrugged his sturdy shoulders and grinned. He wasn't as tall as Jay, but was surely wider and stronger. Working out for the wrestling team had built his already sturdy frame into a tight, strong physique. Jay had noticed before, and that had been instrumental in Jay's growing attraction to him. Wearing a tight, blue shirt and tight jeans, Paul's body was on display, and Jay found himself turned on with fear and worry.

"Cool," Jay said as smoothly and calmly as he could. "What's up?"

Jay began thinking of things he could claim he had to do so that he could get Paul out of the dorm before Sean and Billy arrived in less than half an hour.

Paul said, "Oh, just a boring day. Nothing to do. Kinda wondered what you've been up to lately, so, here I am."

There was something unusual about the way Paul was acting. He seemed different, or nervous, or as if he were hiding something. Jay was sure something was going on, and that worried him even more.

"Well, I got a couple of minutes, but I got to head out soon," Jay said.

"Oh? Got plans?"

"Sure do," Jay said, he hoped convincingly.

"Oh," Paul said with a grimace. "I, uh, was hoping you had some free time today."

"Oh? What's up?"

"Well, I kinda gotta talk to ya about, something. Okay? It's, sorta important. Okay?"

Paul seemed to have more to say, so Jay waited, one eye on the clock. He hoped he could get Paul to spit out whatever it was and get him on his way soon.

"I, uh, fuck. Look, can we go to your room?"

"My roommate's due back soon, but okay," Jay offered,

then stepped back to let Paul in.

Paul walked in, looked around at the small room, and then sat down on the chair at what he could tell was Jay's desk by the pictures and the familiar laptop.

"What's up?" Jay asked again, hoping to get things moving quickly, as he sat on his bed.

"Jay, man, this is, ain't gonna be easy, okay?" Paul said, not looking at him.

"If you're here to tell me you figured out I'm a fag, don't bother," Jay said flatly.

He was surprised at himself, but he didn't care, so long as he got Paul out of his room before Sean and Billy arrived. Jay stared at him, open-mouthed.

"Don't act all surprised and shit. You know," Jay said to Paul's surprised expression. "You gotta figured it out by now."

Jay was surprised at himself, and it was clear that Paul was surprised as well.

"I... " Paul stammered.

"Yeah, well, if that's all you came to tell me, you can go."

Jay held his calm, emotionless expression, but only with extreme effort. He still couldn't believe he had said that. He was angry at himself now, and wanted nothing more than for Paul to leave.

As Jay stood to tell Paul that he could leave, Paul stood and stepped closer to Jay. Jay backed quickly and almost tripped over the throw rug. Paul stopped still and stared at Jay.

"You can leave," Jay repeated without looking at Paul, then turned toward the door.

As Jay's hand closed over the doorknob, he was spun around by Paul's strong arms, then he found himself being held by his forearms in Paul's nearly crushing grip.

"What did you say?" Paul demanded, nearly in Jay's face.

Paul didn't look angry at all, and his tone wasn't angry either, but his words had been loud and forceful. Jay was worried and scared, and now he hoped that Sean and Billy arrived very soon. Jay's mind played out his fate for him in bloody, gruesome detail.

"What did you say?" Paul demanded again, shaking Jay almost roughly.

"I said you can leave! You don't have to tell me you know

I'm a... that I'm... I'm a fag. Okay?"

Now he had gone too far, and now Jay knew that everyone back home would know very soon. It was all over. His parents would hear by the end of the day.

"You're gay?" Paul asked, stunned.

Jay could only nod, hoping that he didn't start bawling like a baby.

"You're... you?" Paul asked, letting go of Jay's arms.

Jay nodded again, now unable to look at Paul at all. He was ashamed and frightened.

The sound of the door opening startled them both. Jay almost fainted and ended up stumbling forward a step, nearly into Paul.

"Jay?" Paul asked.

Jay couldn't respond. He knew who was at the door, and he knew it was now all over and was about to end in the worst way possible.

"Jay, time to take it like a-" Billy said as he started in. "Oh, you got company. Didn't know."

"Hey," Paul said.

"Hi," Billy replied. "Is everything okay, Jay?"

"Oh, yeah. We, uh, this a friend from home," Sean said as casually as he could manage.

"Hi," Paul said, waving. "I'm Paul."

"Billy."

There was a long, awkward silence.

"So, ummm, we still on for this weekend at your cabin?" Billy asked awkwardly.

"Oh, yeah," Jay said, still stunned.

"Goin' to the cabin? Mind if I tag along?" Paul asked.

"You won't want to," Jay said, barely able to stumble to his bed, reeling.

"Why's that?" Sean asked, having walked in at that moment. He closed the door behind himself.

"I told him I'm gay," Jay offered. "You guys know, so no big deal. But he just found out."

Silence.

"I knew he was figuring it out, so I told him. So if you guys don't wanna go to the cabin, I'll understand."

As far as Jay was concerned, that was all he needed to say, and they would all leave. He only hoped they left without Paul convincing Sean and Billy that they needed to teach the fag a lesson. He knew Sean and Billy would pound him as badly as Paul would to cover for themselves. Jay was ready. He had always known it would come to something like this, that it would only be a matter of time.

Now, it was time.

The silence continued.

"What if I said I don't give a fuck?" Sean said firmly.

"Me neither," Billy added. "Jay's a decent guy. I don't care if he is."

"And, if you got a problem with it, maybe I got a problem with you," Sean said menacingly at Paul.

"Me?" Paul gasped. "Have a problem with it?"

Several seconds went by as Jay wondered if it would be possible that this wouldn't end up as badly as he feared.

"I don't," Paul went on. "At all."

"Good," Sean said. "Jay's a good guy, and if anyone caused him any problems, Billy and me, we wouldn't like it."

"Shit!" Paul exclaimed loudly enough that the spell of fear and dread holding Jay motionless was broken, and Jay finally looked up, away from the carpet.

Sean, Billy, and Paul were facing each other, less than a foot between them all, and around Jay in a semi-circle. Jay didn't know what to think, or how to feel. Or what was going on.

"Shit!" Paul repeated. "I mean, shit!"

"What the hell's your problem?" Sean asked, obviously confused.

"You guys are really his friends? Not just, I don't know, not just, like, being tutored by him or something?"

"You saying we're stupid?" Billy asked angrily.

"Fuck no! I'm, I'm asking if you guys are really his friends. Really, friends. And you don't care if he's... gay?"

After three seconds of silence, in which Jay felt as if years had passed, Sean said, "Yes. Jay's a friend. And I was serious about anyone fuckin' with him, too."

"Ditto," Billy added.

Jay choked up, hoping that he didn't sob or cry. No one had ever said anything like that about him before. No one had ever stood up for him before.

"I came here to tell him that I, to apologize for..." Paul

dropped to the couch next to Jay and went on, "Jay, I, want to apologize for, how I didn't talk to you this year. I mean, it wasn't anything you did. Honest. I... I didn't want you to get in any shit. Over..."

Paul put a hand on Jay's knee.

"Jay, I didn't want you to have to put up with any shit when everyone found out about me. I didn't want you to... be, the school fag's friend, and be shit on along with me."

Jay looked up and blinked. He tried to think, but all he saw was Paul, his friend from high school, who'd stopped hanging out with him. And he didn't look happy or like he was about to laugh, like he almost always had. Now he looked worried, scared, nervous, and like he was near tears, too. Jay did the only thing he could do.

He fainted.

Jay opened his eyes and wondered when he had fallen asleep. He was expecting Sean and Billy, he remembered, and shot upright.

"Feeling better?" a familiar but long-missing voice asked.

He noticed then that he was lying on the bed, against Paul, and almost sitting in Paul's lap. He quickly moved to sit up but was held back by Paul's powerful arms.

"No, no. No big movements for a few. Sit back and breathe," Paul demanded, pulling Jay back to himself.

Jay felt ridiculous, being held in someone's arms like that, and especially as he remembered what had happened. He looked at the clock and knew that only a few minutes had passed.

"Where's Sean and Billy? And what the hell is going on?"

"They went to get pizza. They'll be back in a while."

"Pizza?!" Jay yelled. "Fucking pizza? What the fuck is going on?"

Jay pulled away and managed to get out of Paul's grip. He knew Paul had released him on purpose. He stood up, weaved a bit, then fell back onto the bed, dizzy and nauseated. He held his head in his hands, reeling.

"Told you," Paul said gently. "You gotta sit or lay down a couple minutes."

"What the fuck is going on?" he demanded again.

"Sit back, and I promise I fill ya in. Okay?"

Jay let himself fall back onto the bed, hands still over his face. He felt Paul move closer, then a hand on his shoulder.

"You feeling okay?" Paul asked, again very gently. After Jay nodded, Paul began, "Jay, I knew I was gay before high school. Okay, I didn't, know, but I knew. Sorta. I mean, it didn't show up one day, and I started liking... not girls. Okay?"

"You don't have to tell me how it is. I know how it is. I want to know what the fuck is going on here!"

Jay dropped his hands and glared at Paul.

"Were we friends?" Paul asked, meeting Jay eye to eye.

Jay nodded.

"Then listen. I didn't want to get found out, and have someone who was nice to me get called a fag, too. So I didn't talk to you. So you wouldn't be bothered for knowing the fag, in case I got found out. Okay?"

Jay nodded.

"So, I was thinking a lot this last few weeks. And, I miss you. A lot."

Paul swallowed with difficulty, and Jay easily noticed that, being familiar with the same thing in himself.

"So, I came to tell you. I hoped you'd be okay with it, and at least not hate me."

Jay nodded, also familiar with that in himself.

"Maybe even, we could be friends again."

Jay laughed then. The absurdity of the situation was more than he could handle without humor to deal with it. All he could do was laugh. So he did. At first, Paul looked as if he was going to become angry, or upset, but a grin finally cracked his worried frown, and soon he was laughing as well.

When Sean and Billy returned, opening the door without knocking, they saw Jay on the bed, his back against Paul's chest, and Paul's arms around him.

Paul immediately removed his arms and looked ready to stand up. When Jay didn't move, Paul looked worried, nervous, and scared.

"So, you guys didn't kill each other, I see," Sean said, placing a pizza box on the desk and sitting down.

Billy opened the box and took out a slice, as he said, "Looks like they might want to do something else to each other, though," with a laugh.

"So you guys okay?" Sean asked as he grabbed a slice of

the pizza.

Jay laughed once and shook his head. It didn't seem real. Sean and Billy, two popular jocks at college, and Paul, another jock, in his room, together, on purpose, and not a one of them was about to beat him up or call him a fag. Not only that, they were all gay, too. And Paul had proved that he was caring and gentle, and very much liked him. How could any of it be real, let alone all of it?

"I guess," Paul said tentatively.

"Jay? You, uh, mention anything?" Sean asked.

Jay knew exactly what 'anything' Sean meant. He shook his head.

"Want to?" Sean asked tentatively.

"Up to you. I don't care."

"No, up to you."

Jay nodded, then looked back over his shoulder at Paul for a moment.

"Not like Paul wants to go steady or some shit. He just, wanted me to know, that's all. And, he likes me. Sorta."

Paul turned very red, now unable to look anywhere but at the far wall or the ceiling.

"Oh? Going to be exclusive?" Sean asked with a grin.

"No!" Paul said quickly. "I mean, not like that. I, just wanted him to know, about me. That's all. And, that, I… think… he's nice."

"So, it's okay if we pick up where we left off. With me, anyway. And Paul said if there was somebody I was being with, he didn't care, just so long as we were friends."

"Cool," Sean said as he reached for another slice of the pizza. "So, any chance he might, wanna, join us?"

Sean took a bite, Billy choked on his, and Paul asked, "What?"

When Jay was done laughing, which took a few seconds, he sat up and turned to face Paul.

"Uh, Paul, um, Sean and Billy, and, uh me, we, uh, been, um, well… "

"You have not!" Paul said, sitting up in astonishment and staring around at the three of them, wide-eyed and open-mouthed.

"Just this week. I mean, I guess, Sean kinda figured me out. That was why I was sure you had, too, and was why you came over."

"You guys…" Jay began, staring at Billy and Sean.

Both boys grinned, and Billy blushed darkly around his awkward grin.

"You mean… not just me? Not just Jay?" Paul asked, stunned.

Sean shrugged, then Billy followed suit. Both boys continued eating pizza as if watching a movie.

"And you…" Paul began, looking at Jay. "With…" he asked, looking at Sean and Billy. "For real?" he asked, again looking at Jay.

Jay blushed further and nodded, grinning, and wondering how things could change so quickly.

Paul gasped repeatedly, which made the three other boys laugh.

Paul met Sean's eyes and asked, "You?"

Sean nodded.

Paul met Billy's eyes, and before he asked, Billy nodded.

Paul looked at Jay, who shrugged.

"We're all…?"

Three nodding heads answered his unspoken question.

"I… I don't fucking believe this," Paul said in nearly a whisper, as if to himself.

"You don't?" Jay asked. "This time last weekend I was…" he coughed and blushed.

"Still a total and complete virgin," Sean finished for him with a laugh.

"Ass," Jay mumbled with a small laugh.

"Yeah, it was too, but not anymore," Billy said, reaching for another piece of pizza.

"Ass!" Jay said much louder this time, and around Sean and Paul's laughter.

"Oh my God! You got laid before I did?" Paul asked in disbelief.

"Yeah, who'd a figured, huh?" Jay said, trying not to laugh even harder. He stopped in mid-laugh when what Paul had said fully registered. "Wait a sec. What about Nancy Wright?"

"Nothing happened," Paul said with a shrug. "I just went out with her so I…"

All three nodded knowingly.

"So, another virgin to break in, boss," Billy said with a leer.

"If he's willing. And he can take it," Sean said smoothly.

"Willing…to what? Take what?" Paul asked suspiciously.

Three boys grinned. One looked worried.

"Remember how we used to wrestle around? And you'd get my arm or leg up behind me or something, until I cried uncle?" Jay asked Paul.

"Uh, sure," Paul answered cautiously, blushing furiously.

"Well, you can always cry uncle," Jay said, then bounced his eyebrows.

"Cry uncle?" Paul asked.

Jay snickered slightly and turned redder. Sean coughed and threw a crust into the lid of the pizza box.

"You might not like the same thing Jay does. I get the feeling you wouldn't."

"What does Jay like?" Paul asked, his black eyes turning toward Jay questioningly.

Jay got even redder and looked down at his lap.

"Jay likes being… dominated," Sean said, watching Paul closely with his dark green eyes.

"Dominated? Like S and M?" Paul asked in obvious surprise.

"Not so much what you think," Sean said, leaning forward. "He likes being told what to do, and made to do it, and being a little worried and afraid he might be hurt. He's not into pain or anything."

"Well," Jay said with a small grin. "Not much pain, anyway."

"What are you guys into?" Paul asked, now looking a little worried.

"It's not what it sounds like," Jay said. "I… I just like, being a little scared. I guess."

He was obviously embarrassed, and he couldn't believe this conversation was taking place. It was strange enough to him that these three guys were all gay, but talking about sex, and not only just sex, but how he liked being scared and maybe a little hurt, was shocking. He was about as embarrassed as he could remember being, at least, with his clothes on. He literally squirmed against Paul on the bed, still sitting almost in his lap.

"Jay just likes a little threat. And a little slapping and pinching. Nothing extreme. Just a little light fun, to keep him on his toes," Sean explained. "I'm wondering if you do, too."

"Hell no!" Paul said firmly.

Jay visibly deflated.

"No, I think he'd like being in charge," Billy said. "He's a butch type."

Paul grinned but tried to hide it.

"Ah," Sean said, grinning wider now. "I see. You'd like knowing you're in charge, huh?"

"So?" Paul said, now the embarrassed one.

"I got an idea," Sean said gleefully. "You up for some fun this weekend?"

"Like what?" Paul asked quickly.

Jay could feel Paul tensing, but wasn't sure why. He couldn't see behind him to Paul's face, not without some contortions and being obvious.

"You horny?" Sean asked.

"You're kidding?" Paul asked, understanding Sean's intent now. "The four of us?"

Jay had felt Paul's erection against his lower back earlier, and now he was sure it was rising again. He grinned.

"No, I'm not. I think it'd be fun. See, I'll take charge of Jay, 'cause I know what I'm doing, and you take charge of Bill, and he'll make sure you don't make any big mistakes. And you follow my lead. I think it'd be really fun."

"And do what?" Paul asked, obviously curious and interested.

"Play," Sean said simply. "And we've got some interesting toys, too."

Billy laughed softly.

"What toys?" Paul asked.

"Now, don't ruin the surprise!" Sean said gleefully. "Just, are you interested?"

Jay could easily tell that he was, as his interest was poking against the small of his back as he reclined in Paul's lap.

"Maybe," Paul answered timidly.

"If you don't like it, we can stop and just get down to some standard stuff. Get each other off that way. I won't mind a bit. I'm curious to see what you've got in those jeans, anyway," Sean said with a big grin, his green eyes glinting.

Paul grinned wider, ran a hand through his black hair, and turned a little darker red.

"Come on, Paul. It's fun," Jay said, turning his head to look up and back at Paul.

Paul met his brown eyes and smiled.

"So long as I get to play with that monster of yours," he said, blushing even darker.

"We can switch once you get the idea," Sean said. "You can take over on Jay, and I'll show you how much Bill likes his pain."

"Are we really gonna do this?" Paul asked.

"Please?" Jay almost begged.

Jay stretched up and around, and managed to pull Paul's head down so that he could kiss him. It was the most daring thing he had ever done. But he had liked Paul for a long time, and this was too good to pass up. He would do anything to have Paul. He didn't mind if Sean was first, so long as he got to watch and be there. And the idea of switching, and having Paul in charge of him, had him tingling all over.

Their kisses went from light, exploratory briefness, to heavy, deep, long ones. Their breathing increased. Sean and Billy could hear that, and they grinned at each other as they nodded.

Chapter 6

"Okay, you guys," Sean said. "Break it up."

Jay and Paul grinned in embarrassment once they stopped kissing.

"We're wasting time. How long is the drive, Jay?" Sean asked.

"About... three hours?"

"Then we better be heading out. I've got a few things to pack, and Billy does as well," Sean said.

"I'll be back in about fifteen minutes," Billy said, standing. "Don't leave without me!"

"I don't have time to go home, so I guess I'll have to do without trunks," Paul said.

"We won't be doing much swimming," Sean said, grinning wickedly.

Jay and Paul blushed darker, grinning awkwardly at each other. Sean retrieved the overnight bag from his locked footlocker as Jay threw a change of clothes into his backpack. Jay sat next to Paul as Sean packed clothes into his own backpack, grinning awkwardly at Paul who did much the same back at him. Sean grinned at them both, laughing at times.

"How many bedrooms does this cabin have?" Sean asked.

"Two," Jay answered. "And we'll have to make the beds. The blankets and things aren't on them when no one is there."

That's fine," Sean said. "You sure your folks won't show up?"

"Sure. They're at someone's wedding this weekend in California. Some cousin of Mom's she hasn't seen in ages. They're flying there and then back on Sunday night."

"Good. Then this should be a wild weekend!" Sean said, his

grin widening.

"We're really going to do this?" Paul asked Jay, obviously still quite surprised.

Jay snickered, then said, "I hope so!" his blush darkening further.

Paul leaned closer to Paul, grinning and snickering. Paul laughed, then leaned in and kissed Jay. They returned to kissing passionately as Sean watched. When Billy returned, Paul and Jay broke apart.

"Let's get going!" Sean said. "What kind of car do you have, Paul? Will we all fit?"

"Yeah, we'll all fit," Paul said. "I think I remember the way, too."

"Then let's get going. We can stop on the way for some grub and pick up some stuff to have at the cabin."

The four of them walked casually to Paul's car. Outwardly, they looked like four young college students heading out for a weekend trip.

They stopped at White Castle, then picked up groceries. Within half-an-hour, they were on the highway headed out of town. Just under three hours later, they pulled up in front of a rustic, one-story cabin on an isolated rut of a road, not having passed another car or structure for twenty minutes. Trees pressed close to the log cabin on three sides, the fourth side open to the view of the rocky shore and the lake.

"Nice place," Billy said as they piled out of the car. "And no neighbors."

"Nearest is along the shore about two miles," Jay said, pulling his backpack from the trunk.

"So we can skinny-dip?" Sean asked, grinning.

Jay blushed darkly, grinned, and nodded.

Sean began taking off his shirt.

"You might want to keep your shoes on until you get to the water," Jay offered. "The shore is all rocks."

"We can swim later," Billy said, smiling. "I want to get started. Paul's hot, and I want to have a look."

Paul snickered. Jay actually dug at the ground with the toe of his shoe like a small schoolboy.

"Okay," Sean agreed. "Let's get inside."

Jay led them to the door, removed the key from a board along the porch, and then led them inside. They tossed their packs aside and then carried the groceries into the kitchen.

They took sodas into the front room and sat down, Paul and Jay on the couch, Sean and Billy pulling two chairs next to each other.

They talked about the cabin, and Jay shared some memories of summers there, particularly the week that Paul came with Jay and his parents. It wasn't long before Jay and Paul were sitting close, smiling at each other.

"We could have had an even better time this time," Paul hinted, snickering.

Jay blushed darkly, snickered, and nodded. They leaned close and kissed.

"You guys warm up, we'll go set up," Sean said, standing.

"Set up?" Paul asked, pulling back from kissing Jay.

"Some things we want to get ready. You guys take a few minutes and make out. No taking anything off, or putting any hands inside any clothes, though," Sean ordered.

Jay nodded, grinning widely, still breathing hard, and said, "Use the room on the right."

As Billy and Sean walked toward the bedroom door, packs in hands, Jay and Paul returned to learning how to kiss each other.

Jay was excited and growing even more so. He felt his heart hammering and his blood rushing through his neck. Kissing Paul was intensely thrilling, and he couldn't believe it was really happening. A part of his mind detached and looked back over the events of the past few days, wondering at the luck and the pure happiness. Now, with Paul involved too, it was beyond his wildest hopes and dreams.

Three guys at the same time! He thought in wonder. And one is Paul! Fucking awesome!

Paul's hands started roaming across his chest and found his nipples. They were hard and extremely sensitive. Paul's strong, blunt fingers rolled and pinched them, making Jay whimper and gasp.

Jay turned so that he was facing Paul, and his hand found Paul's nipple on his broad, powerful chest. He rubbed small circles around it as they returned to kissing deeply. Paul found that he liked that a great deal, especially from Jay. His breathing increased further.

Paul reached down and followed Jay's thigh up to his groin,

where he easily found the length of his hardness inside of his jeans. Jay gasped softly as Paul's fingers explored its length and thickness. Hurriedly, Jay found Paul's erection, and toyed with it, too.

"Oh, gawd, I want you so bad!" Paul gasped. "You're so hot! I want to play with this thing so bad!"

He began unzipping Jay's jeans, but Jay slapped his hand and then pulled it away.

"No. Sean said not to."

"Fuck that. I want to see it at least!"

"No!" Jay said firmly. "He said not to take anything off or reach inside."

"You're taking his orders seriously?" Paul asked, looking into Jay's brown eyes with his black ones.

"Yes. It makes it more fun. He knows what he's doing. Okay?"

Paul sighed, relenting.

"Better be worth it. I'm dying to get in your pants!"

"I can't wait, either. But we will."

Jay slammed his lips back onto Paul's.

They were still kissing when they heard a cough. They broke apart quickly to see Billy standing naked at the start of the hallway. His bare chest was nearly pure white, with large, pink nipples standing out like candies against his milky skin, just the barest visible red hair between them. He was lean and strong, and his pink and red cock pointed upward, his red sack hanging below. His bright red patch of pubic hair stood out against his very pale skin. His cock bounced slightly with each beat of his heart.

"Come on, it's time, noobs."

He grinned nicely and waved at them to follow him. He turned, and both boys watched him, admiring his buttocks. They looked at each other, then grinned.

"He's got a nice ass," Paul said.

"His best feature. I could do without the red hair, though."

"I like it," Paul said with a short laugh.

"Come on," Jay said, standing up.

Paul looked directly at Jay's lap, grinning.

"Damn!"

Jay's erection stretched to the side of his jeans, well into the area for the pocket. Jay laughed and put his hands over it.

"You can come and see it," he said, then turned to follow Billy.

"Damned right!"

They laughed as they ran into the bedroom. Sean and Billy were both naked, standing together face to face, kissing and running their hands up and down each other's sides and backs.

"Oh, wow," Paul said softly.

"Hot, huh?" Jay asked him.

"Like, yeah!"

Sean and Billy separated.

"Woah!" Paul cried out, his eyes growing large.

"What?" Jay asked.

"Sean! He's almost as massive as you! I think."

"Thanks," Sean said, grabbing his long dick and waggling it. "But first, you both get undressed by us. Now, come stand here."

As he sat down, Sean indicated a spot just to the left of the middle of the bed, right at the edge, directly in front of Billy, and said, "You here, Paul. You, here," Sean said to Jay, pointing at the floor directly in front of himself.

When Jay stood in front of Sean, and Paul stood in front of Billy, both Billy and Sean reached out and began touching and exploring the groins in front of them. Jay and Paul grinned at each other, nearly laughing, neither of them believing what was happening.

"Now, the real secret to real fun is to take your time. Go slow and easy. Lots of teasing and touching," Sean said, as his hands explored Jay's erection and his butt.

Billy said, "Take time to build up some energy. And a big load. And relax and enjoy it." He looked up at Paul as he explored his package, and said, "I like strong, buff guys. You're hot. And you have a great ass. I can't wait to have some fun with it."

His hands slid around to cup and massage Paul's buttocks. Paul sighed deeply and audibly. He had never been touched before, not even on the few dates he had gone on with Nancy. The feeling of Billy's hands playing with his butt made him almost shiver. His cock was so hard it nearly hurt, and his balls ached.

Billy gave his cheeks a very firm squeeze, then a hard slap.

"If I hurt you too much, say so, otherwise I'm gonna go

further as we go along. Until you say that's your limit. I might even go past that after you say so, just to test your real limits. Don't get offended or anything. I'm just trying to make this as fun as possible. Okay?"

"Okay. I get it, I think. You want to see how much I like, and you'll do more sometimes to make sure I wasn't kidding."

"And to make it hurt, too. Sometimes that really heats things up. But if I go too far, you let me know, without getting all bitchy. It's all meant to be fun, that's all."

"Okay. Just don't go getting crazy. Or I'll bust you one."

"I'd probably like that," Billy said, grinning widely.

"He does love his pain," Sean said, his hands running all over Jay's body. "He loves pain. You'll see."

"What kind of pain?" Paul asked.

"You'll see," Sean said in a sing-song.

"I don't think you'll be up to my level. But we'll find yours," Billy cooed, then slapped Paul's ass hard with both hands.

"If that's what you call pain, you're a wuss," Paul said.

"Just gettin' started. Like I said, we'll build up as we go," Billy said, then moved his hands to the front of Paul's pants and slapped Paul in the groin.

"Ow!"

"Just gettin' started," Billy said with a leering grin.

Sean's hands had moved all over Jay, then pushed his shirt up. Jay leaned down with his arms over his head so that Sean could remove the shirt. Paul and Billy did much the same.

"Oh, man, what a nice set of pecs," Billy said admiringly at Paul.

His hands roamed over Paul's big, brown nipples, and pinched and twisted them firmly. Paul winced but remained quiet, grinning as well.

"And a nice trail, too," Billy said, then began kissing and licking the trail and the slight patch around his navel.

Paul snickered and grinned. He looked at Jay as Sean did exactly the same things to him.

"Are we allowed to touch each other?" Paul asked.

"Nope. Keep your hands to yourself," Sean said between tonguing Jay's navel and kissing his stomach.

"Damn," Paul said firmly. "This could suck."

"Not yet, just hands and lips right now," Billy said, using

his on Paul's abdomen. "You are fucking buff, dude!"

Paul snickered, and then said, "Thanks. You ain't bad yourself."

"You looked, huh?"

"Oh, hell yeah. Nice fuckin' bod, man."

"Thanks," Billy said, then bit the edge of Paul's navel.

"Yeow!" Paul snapped.

"That didn't hurt that much," Billy said, as if scolding a child.

"Surprised, mostly."

"I bet your cock jumped," Sean said, laughing. "Probably squeezed out a nice drop of pre-jizz."

Paul laughed and turned red.

"You're right," Billy said, grinning up at Paul.

"Geeze. You guys that experienced?"

"We've been fucking each other since sixth grade," Billy said, obviously bragging.

"No fucking way!" Paul exclaimed.

"Hell yes, fucking way," Sean declared.

Sean then sucked Jay's navel firmly, making squeaking sounds. Jay snickered and bent forward.

"Can I put my hands on your shoulders?" Jay asked.

"Go ahead. And get ready for something weird," Sean said with a leer.

Jay made a half-grimace of fear, then grinned widely. He was shivering inside, and they were beginning to move through his body and become obvious. He loved that shiver, and knew it came only from the fear that Sean was so good at giving him.

Sean kissed and sucked his navel and treasure trail, and Jay loved it. The tickling felt great. Sean's hot breath on his wet skin also felt very good. And Sean's hands roamed, often playing with one or another of his sensitive nipples. They were very hard now, and even the slightest touch sent strong, nearly electric waves deep into his gut and through to his spine.

Sean's hands tugged upward on the waist of his jeans, rotating them side to side slightly. Then again. And again. Each time pulling the crotch of the jeans higher and tighter around his cock and balls. Then Sean stood up and pulled the jeans up so hard that he lifted Jay's feet off the ground.

"Aw, fuck!" Jay cried out.

One of his balls had been caught and was pinched by the seam, and it hurt. A lot.

"You crushed a nut!" Jay complained.

Sean kept snugging the jeans upward, turning them as well, and his nut slipped sideways. The sudden relief and the weird sensation made Jay shudder and groan. Sean released his jeans and sat back down.

"Back in place, and hands to your sides," Sean said firmly, grinning.

Jay stepped gingerly back into place, then dropped his arms, grinning.

"Still hurt?" Sean asked.

"Sort of. Going to a while, I think. Ouch."

"Not bad, though?"

"Sort of, man."

"How hard are you now?"

Jay noticed that his dick was pulsing in rapid time.

"What the hell?"

Sean laughed softly, then placed his hand over the obvious erection for a few moments.

"Nice. Throbbing like a clock," he said.

"How the hell did you learn that?" Jay asked.

"Here and there. Online mostly. And you have to do it just right, or it fucking kills."

"And it does!" Billy attested. "But, I like it either way." When he looked at Paul, he saw a frown. "He didn't really hurt him, dude. You really like Jay, don't you?"

Paul turned a dark red and hid a grin.

"Jay," Billy said. "This guy is really into you."

"Shut the hell up," Paul said in a weakly angry tone.

Jay turned nearly as darkly red as Paul.

"Hey, it's okay. He should know that," Sean said gently. "You got a real admirer," he told Jay.

"Stop it," Jay said weakly, taking short glances at Paul.

Paul took the same short glances at Jay. Billy and Sean glanced at each other, grinning.

Jay was ecstatic to learn that Paul liked him so much. It made him feel wonderful. He had never felt the sense of being wanted like that before. While Sean and Billy had been friends now, they hadn't shown that kind of attraction to Jay, not that he had recognized. The warmth of knowing that Paul really liked him spread through him like a rising tide.

"Don't worry, I won't really hurt him," Sean said to Paul. "I'll just give him what he likes. And you pay attention so you can give it to him too."

Paul sighed in exasperation. Jay laughed softly in embarrassment.

"Stage two," Sean said to Billy.

They unfastened and unzipped their charge's jeans, slowly. They pulled their jeans down and motioned for them to step out of them. Both boys were wearing white briefs, and both boys tented them. While Jay made a long, sideways bulge, nearly to the waistband of his shorts, at nearly a forty-five-degree angle and against his body, Paul made a shorter, blunter tent, outward, and almost directly upward. At the end of both tents, a wet spot was apparent, though Paul had obviously made a much larger one. Both boys filled the bottom of their shorts with their balls, which Sean and Billy cupped and hefted.

Jay's tall, narrow, lean frame contrasted with Paul's shorter, compact and powerful one. While Jay's light hair was sparse and hardly noticeable, Paul's dark hair was thicker and heavier. Jay was pale, too, while Paul had a naturally darker complexion, tanned everywhere except at the top of his thighs, around his privates, and his ass.

Sean and Billy nuzzled their faces into the white material in front of them. Jay and Paul breathed heavily, nearly gasping. They grinned at each other often. And both of them yearned to touch each other.

Their cocks were jumping and bouncing in their shorts under the mouths of Billy and Sean, who moved from cock to balls, and back again, repeatedly. Their wet spots grew in the passing minutes, and their breaths began to race along with their pulses.

Jay began moving his hips, the instinct hard to resist. When Paul saw that, he did the same thing, and found it added to the sexual satisfaction that filled him. He was shuddering now, too, and at times, his head fell back and his eyes rolled up for brief moments as he groaned deep in his chest. Paul loved seeing Jay's body, and watched it as often as he could, but the sexual charge overruled his desires at times, making his head loll back.

"Stage three," Sean said, and then he and Billy helped their charges out of their underwear.

Jay's long cock bounced at first, then steadied, angled slightly upward. Paul's shorter cock hardly moved, and pointed almost forty-five degrees upward, but throbbed gently with his racing heart.

Jay's cock was long, thick, and pale, with a rumpled fold of foreskin behind his smooth head. His balls were large and hung from his body, the skin of the sack pale, with light, sandy blond hairs.

Paul's cock was about six inches, blunt-headed, with prominent coronal edges, and a small, tightly closed opening. His thick head was darkly red, and glistening with leaked fluid. It had a short area behind it, reddish in color, and then a pale shaft into his dense, black bush. His balls were small, the sack reddish and wrinkled, nearly up tight to his body. Black hairs spread out to his thighs, and down to his calves, where they were heavy and dense.

Sean and Billy leaned back, looking at both boys, but taking in the new vista of Paul's naked body the most. Paul's eyes were locked onto Jay's very long and thick cock. He shivered at the sight and ached to reach out and touch it. He didn't like abiding by Sean's rules, but since Jay liked to, he went along.

Jay gazed longingly at Paul's body, mostly at his erection, and also wanted very badly to reach out and play with it. He wasn't disappointed at all in the size. He was glad that it wasn't as large as Sean's or as thick as Billy's. He knew it would be easier to take, and immediately began imagining what it would feel like in his ass.

Sean and Billy began running their hands along the sides of the boys' hips, just grazing along the sides of their bushes. Two cocks jumped and twitched, and soon had clear fluids beading at the holes. While Jay had a fairly large opening, dark, oval, and slightly open, Paul had a small, tight hole, more rounded and tightly closed. Jay's leaked fluid slowly gathered before running under the end of his head. Paul's drops were smaller and fell faster. Each one of each boys' excretions were licked up before they fell away, but no lips touched their sensitive skin. Both cocks danced and jumped at the touch of the warm, soft tongues.

"God! How long does this go on for?" Paul asked, his

frustration clear.

"As long as we want," Sean answered. "But it's time for stage four."

Sean and Billy stood, their cocks hard. Sean's much longer and thinner cock protruded from his dark patch of hair almost horizontally, while Billy's shorter, thicker, pinker cock stood out from his red bush upward at almost a forty-five-degree angle. Both bounced and jumped, and were wet with fluid.

"On your knees, gentlemen," Sean said.

Jay and Paul snickered, grinning at each other, then obeyed.

"Get to it," Billy said. "No hands. And not on yourself, either."

Jay gobbled down Sean's length, moaning around it, bobbing from the start. He loved giving head, and fell into it with gusto, shivering. Sean gasped and placed his hands on Jay's shoulders.

"God damn it! He's so good," Sean crowed.

Paul leaned tentatively forward, his guts churning and tingling. He couldn't believe he was about to suck a cock – finally! He gently wrapped his fingers around the thick, pink cock, feeling the warmth, softness, and the hardness. His stomach rolled over and his dick jerked and leaked more pre-cum. He placed his lips over Billy's pink head. He sucked gently, tasting someone else's pre-cum for the first time. He liked it, and with those first hurdles passed, he moved further down the length of the dick. Billy pushed forward, until all of his cock was inside Paul's mouth. Then he began humping Paul's mouth very slowly.

"Suck it, harder, and change it up. Soft, hard, in between, don't let me guess what's next. And move that tongue all over it," Billy instructed.

Paul obeyed, and soon found himself bobbing and sucking, licking, and liking the smell and taste. He found that the velvety softness of Billy's head was a wonderful sensation. The hardness behind it seemed impossibly contradictory to the softness of the head.

"That's right. Move that tongue. Push it in the hole and swab inside."

Paul did, and sucked as hard as he could.

"Nice!" Billy crooned. "That's right. Get into it. Suck a nice hard cock."

Billy pumped his hips, Paul's lips making loud sucking noises.

"Not bad at all," Billy said encouragingly.

"Jeeze, I'm getting the cum sucked right out of me!" Sean gasped. "Fucking hold up, Jay."

Jay reluctantly stopped. He watched Paul bob up and down on Billy's thrusting cock, and his own cock released a large tide of pre-cum as it twitched and jumped. His body shook as a wave of warm sexual energy washed through it. He was breathing hard and fast, and wanted nothing as badly as he wanted to reach out and grab Paul's dick or caress his ass.

"He's hot, huh?" Sean asked him.

Jay snapped his head to see Sean watching him. He laughed and nodded.

"He sure is. I can't wait!"

"Awww, man," Billy said, the shudders in his voice coming across clearly. "He's not bad at all, especially for his first head."

Billy thrust a few more times, then said, "Okay, hold up."

Paul slid off the thick, pink cock and grinned up at Billy. Then he looked at Sean and Jay. He couldn't believe this. He was as turned on as he had ever been. His body shivered and his insides felt like boiling lava. He panted and grinned. He thought Jay had never looked so cute. His soft lips were wet and dark, fuller than normal, and his sparkling brown eyes were deep and warm. He moved his eyes down Jay's body, loving everything he saw. The leanness, the smoothness, the largeness between his thighs.

"Okay, guys. Let's have some real fun," Sean said.

He and Billy positioned the other two boys in the middle of the bed, nearly side by side, and they arranged Paul and Jay with their legs out straight and wide apart. Sean picked up his overnight bag then and sat in front of Jay. Billy sat in front of Paul. Sean and Billy sat with their knees over the knees of their charges.

Sean opened the bag and pulled out another bag, flat and with a zipper. Then a tube of antiseptic, a tube of lubricant, and a small package of tissues. He placed these things between himself and Billy.

"The spikes of joy," Billy said with reverence.

"The what?" Paul asked.

Sean picked up the little case and unzipped the long zipper all the way around three sides of it. He flipped it open to reveal twelve shiny metal rods. Each had a small, oval tip, each a different size, ranging from about the size of an orange seed to something the size of a very large pill. They were round and oval, and on the end of thin, straight, shiny metal rods with a flat handle.

"These," Sean said, removing one, "Are called sounders. They're made just for what we're going to use them for. And they kick ass."

"Maybe my favorite toys," Billy said with a huge grin.

"What do you do with them?" Paul predictably asked.

"You will soon see," Sean said, grinning.

Sean examined Jay's dick closely, squeezing the tip to open the hole, then looked closely at the heavily protruding tube on the underside.

"I think he'll take the number two easy," Sean said.

"Yup. Gotta go with the number one for Paul here," Billy agreed.

Sean removed a rod from the case, one of the middle-sized ones, and held it up by the flat handle. He held it out for Jay to examine closely. The thin, round, shiny metal rod was about the thickness of the lead core of a pencil. The bead on the end of it was oval, polished to a smooth shine.

"This is the number seven. Billy uses it on me. So, Jay, you're going to use it on me today. But later."

He slid the rod back into its holders.

Billy pulled the next one out of the case, and said, "This is the number eight. It's just a tiny bit larger than the seven Sean just showed you," Billy said as he let Paul examine it up close.

Paul wondered if his hunch was correct, and doubting he would be willing to try this out for anything.

Sean removed the first rod from the other side and held it up.

"This is the number one. The smallest. This one is for Paul, since it's his first time and he has a small opening."

He put it back in the case.

"This," Billy said, "Is the number two. You get it, Jay, because your cock has a nice, wide hole, and your tube is thick, so it'll fit easy."

Billy added a drop of lubricant to the oval bead on the end

of it.

Paul's erection started drooping.

"Do you guys think you're going to do what I think you think you're going to do with those... things?" Paul asked.

Sean and Billy laughed.

"It doesn't hurt. Not a real hurt. Stings some, but man, when you get used to it, it fucking rocks," Billy said.

"I love it, too. Fucking kicks ass," Sean said enthusiastically.

"The hell," Paul said, grimacing.

"Sean and me can do each other first, so you see," Billy offered.

"I'm game," Jay said.

The idea frightened him, so it turned him on intensely. The idea of having something inserted into his urethra was foreign and scary. He knew it couldn't hurt much, or Sean wouldn't like it as much as he said he did. He knew Billy would, but he knew Billy probably preferred the larger ones, too.

"You're serious?" Paul asked him.

Jay nodded.

"You can wait and see how the three of us, Jay especially, take it. Okay?" Sean offered.

Paul nodded. He wasn't keen on this at all, and was sure he'd pass even if Jay liked it.

Sean asked Jay, "You want to be first? It'd be better if you saw and felt how it was done before you tried on me. There's a couple of tricks to it, and I'd be happier if you understood them before you go shoving it me like a skewer."

Jay laughed hard and nodded.

"First, I'm going to lube you. I'll stick the end of the tube into your hole, and push a little lube in. You'll feel a weird feeling, and it'll sort of let you know what to expect when the spike goes in, okay?"

Jay nodded, his body filled with a shivering expectation. He was more than a little ready, even impatient to try it. More pre-cum oozed from his hole as his cock danced in time with his pulse.

"Do not move your hips or your dick. Not even a little. Hold still," Sean said, staring directly into Jay's eyes. "Get me?"

Jay nodded, looking a little concerned now.

"If you jerk around suddenly, it can hurt. Just don't move. Stay very still," Sean advised one last time.

Paul watched closely, moving his eyes from Jay's long, thick cock and what Sean was doing to it, to Jay's cute face and his grinning, slightly grimacing expression. He was tensed to jerk Sean's hand away if Jay yelled or complained, and ready for a fight if needed. He no longer had an erection.

Sean placed the little tip of the tube against Jay's hole and wiggled it inside. It was the strangest feeling Jay had ever felt. It was nothing like he thought it would be. It was pure pleasure, only a hint of discomfort, until Sean squeezed the tube. Then a heavy pressure grew, as if he were trying to pee but the end of his dick was pinched closed. And as the lubricant moved deeper into his urethra, the sensation grew and intensified. He shivered and gasped. Sean removed the tube and the pressure left, but the weird feeling deeper in his dick remained.

"Okay?" Sean asked.

"Fucking wild," Jay said with a grin.

Sean pinched the tip of his cock closed, then began firmly rubbing his thick tube downward, pushing the lubricant deeper.

"That doesn't hurt?" Paul asked.

"Yes, but not bad. Almost nothing. Weird as fuck, kinda nice."

Paul was surprised.

Sean moved his fingers repeatedly down the underside of Jay's long cock. He began at the tip each time, encouraging the lubricant deeper and deeper. When he reached the place where the thick tube continued beneath the front of Jay's sack, Jay wriggled and gasped. Sean continued, working the thick tube through Jay's scrotum until he began working along the tube behind Jay's sack. He followed it as far as he could, and Jay squirmed and gasped.

"Okay, now, we're going to take this slow. And it's going to be weird at first. No moving at all! So get comfortable. Lean back onto your hands again."

Jay nodded, wiggled down in place, and nodded again.

Sean held Jay's cock with his free hand and pointed it directly upward. It throbbed gently with Jay's heartbeat. He placed the rounded tip of the rod against the slightly open hole of Jay's head and rotated it. Jay groaned a bit as the little oval bead on the end began entering his hole.

Paul nearly gasped as the shiny oval began to disappear inside of Jay's opening. Jay did gasp, but not in pain, and his grin turned into a near grimace. Paul readied to pull the thing out of Jay and shove it into Sean's eye if Jay cried out in pain.

"The trick is to always let it go in on its own, never push it except the tiniest little bit, so fucking careful. It's sensitive in there and you have to be careful not to push much at all," Billy explained. "Sean's a master at it, so don't worry," he added to Paul's concerned expression.

The entire oval tip vanished, and Jay gasped an, "Oh-my-God-so-cool!" very softly as visible tremors ran through his thighs. His back arched. He gasped more as the visible length of the thin rod began getting shorter. Sean's fingers followed the progress of the oval tip into Jay's tube, and when more than an inch was inside and he felt the first resistance at the first bending, he stopped.

"How's that?" he asked.

"Fucking wild as hell!" Jay exclaimed, his voice quivering.

"Doesn't hurt?" Paul asked again, looking concerned.

"Fuck yes! Tiny little stings! Wild! Love it! Oh, man!"

"It gets more sensitive from here. There's a little bend in your tube, and I'm right at it. This might sting more, so let me know if it's too much."

Jay nodded enthusiastically.

With his fingers, Sean could feel the exact location of the little bead through Jay's thick tube. He all but let go of the handle with his other hand, letting the full weight of the object rest inside of Jay's urethra. It barely moved, so Sean ever so slightly rotated the flat handle. It slid almost immediately and Sean let the weight of it drag it down, feeling its progress with his other fingers.

"Fucking master," Billy sighed.

"Ho-o-oly... shi-i-i-it," Jay groaned from deep inside.

Delicious tingles fired outward from the depths of his cock like he had never known. The strange and intense pressure and sensation seemed to cause his whole body to fill with those incredible shivers.

All three boys could easily see Jay's body shuddering powerfully as his head flopped backward.

"Aw-w-w-w-w," Jay gasped, long and shivering.

His shoulders shuddered as if he were on the edge of freezing to death. Even his biceps and thighs shuddered deeply along with his breaths.

"Okay?" Sean asked.

"Oh... God... yes!" Jay panted.

Most of the instrument was inside now, and Paul goggled. Jay was clearly enjoying it, and it was amazing to watch, so his cock began surging upward.

Jay was deep in pleasure. He had luxuriated in the sensations of his prostate being massaged, but this was even more intense and incredibly powerful. The slight pain and the extreme pleasure were mixing in huge proportions, and his body was quivering from head to toes. The cold metal sent shivers through the inside of his thick, long cock, and as it slid deeper, it was as if it fired a set of nerves he never knew existed. Nerves that were exquisitely sensitive and wildly erotic. His cock swelled as if it were in mid-orgasm every second, pulsing tightly. He couldn't control his breathing, and his entire body shuddered from inside out. His major muscles shivered, as if he were in a deep freezer, naked and wet. The stinging, burning, stretching feeling of the bead sliding into him was easily the best thing he had ever felt.

Sean felt the rod halt at the next slight bend at the base of Jay's cock near his scrotum. He saw Jay jerk.

"Oh-my-God!" Jay gasped.

"Hurt?" Paul asked again.

"Yes! But it hurts so good! Fuckin' yes!"

"It hurts?" Paul asked yet again.

"It's not really hurting. It just feels so fucking incredible! It feels so wild and so fuckin' great that it hurts how much it feels so good!"

Sean snickered.

"It's just fucking incredible," Billy said. "Don't worry. We won't hurt him. Or you. It's not about that. It's about how fucking awesome it feels."

Paul was still concerned. The very idea was almost insane. He didn't see how it could feel anything but uncomfortable, at least, if not just plain painful.

"It's at another bend, Jay. Need to encourage it again. Okay?"

"Yeah!"

Sean and Billy laughed. Paul looked confused and worried. Jay felt the delicious pressure begin behind his balls. His long, thick cock twitched around the rod as Sean held it very still.

"Aw, I'm gonna," Jay grunted deeply.

"No, just hold still," Sean advised him, not moving the long cock or the wand.

More than a minute passed as Jay quivered strongly, on the edge of a strong orgasm. It welled up and threatened, his body shivering and expecting release. But it slowed, ebbed, and receded over that long minute. His cock twitched less and less, and his body began a slower, steady vibration.

When Jay's breath steadied and his cock stabilized, Sean asked, "Pass?"

Jay nodded, grinning expansively, and shuddered once.

"Fuckin' thought I was gonna."

"Oh, you were. But we put it off for now. But not for long. Ready to go again?"

Jay nodded vigorously.

"We're at a bend, so I have to encourage it a little," Sean explained.

"Fucking shove the thing in!" Jay almost screamed.

"Not gonna do that. Just gonna let my finger rest on the top of it. And remember, hold very, very still. Especially now that it's so far in."

Sean bent Jay's cock downward a little, then turned the flat handle, and Jay shuddered violently with a loud gasp, his head going back on his neck. Sean released the wand, and it stayed where it was. He twisted it slowly, then let his finger rest on the end of the flat handle, and the instrument slid further in. Jay gasped in a deep, shuddering breath. That pressure mounted and his body jerked.

"Oh-ho-ho-ho-ho-ho," Jay shuddered, then sucked in another loud, gasping breath.

The instrument slid in deeper, slowly, with each shudder of Jays' body and each pulsing throb of his long cock. Sean felt the little bud nearing Jay's scrotum through the heavy tube on the underside of his thick cock.

Jay's head was still back on his neck, and his body shuddered deeply. His breath shook with the convulsions of his major muscles. His skin broke out in heavy goosebumps.

"It just slides in like that?" Paul asked incredulously.

"Mostly. You saw me help it some. But yeah, as long as you don't use a bigger one, it goes right in on its own. You just need to guide it and sometimes help it," Sean explained.

As Jay's cock pulsed deeply, again and again, in time with his rapid heartbeat, the metal rod slid deeper with each one.

"Oh-my-God!" Jay gasped when his cock throbbed deeply and his head darkened. "Going to!"

Sean stopped the wand and held the fat, long cock steady.

"Breathe deep and try not to," he told Jay.

Jay nodded and whimpered, trying to relax and prevent the swelling and rising tide. The sensation of the bud deep in his cock was overwhelmingly pleasant and nearly painful, and he knew any motion of it would cause him to explode. He held still, and Sean held his cock and the wand still, and the growing pressure relented over another long, slow minute.

When he relaxed a bit, and his cock no longer throbbed, he sighed deeply.

"Over?" Sean asked.

Jay nodded, his head still back on his neck. He was filled with delicious tingles and waves and slid deeper inside of himself under the wonderful sensations.

Sean relaxed his grip on the flat handle and the wand slowly slid downward again, making Jay shudder deeply and he let out a long, deep, shuddering moan. Slowly, with each swelling and warping of Jay's massive cock, the device slid deeper. Over a minute later, the flat handle came to rest at the opening of his hole, and Sean moved his fingers away from it. With his other fingers, he felt the little bud through his scrotum. He was amazed. Even with his long cock, he had never taken the whole length of a sounding rod before hitting the tight bend behind his balls.

"All in," he said in awe.

Billy whispered, "So fucking cool!"

Jay's head snapped down and he opened his eyes. The sight of the handle at the end of his dick was startling and bizarre.

"Wow," he breathed.

"What's it like?" Paul asked.

"Paul! You got to do this! It's like nothing else! Wow!"

"Seriously?"

Jay grinned ear to ear, nodding.

"Check this," Sean said, then gingerly slid a fingernail along the rough, wide side of the handle, sending vibrations through it.

"Oh, yes!" Jay grunted. "Fuckin' Aiy!"

Jay felt his balls retract and his anus clench. The pressure began building again. His outstretched legs below Sean's tensed and relaxed in waves that were out of his control.

Sean gently gripped the handle and slowly rotated it.

"Oh my God!" Jay nearly screamed as his upper body twisted.

"Remember to keep your hips and dick stationary," Sean warned.

Jay nodded, almost too far gone to hear him.

Sean pulled very gently and slowly on the handle, pulling an inch of the instrument out of Jay.

"Don't take it out!" Jay pleaded.

"Not all the way. Relax and enjoy this."

Sean pulled slowly, watching Jay's body shudder even more in reaction, until the bead came to the bend just inside his hole. Then he let it slide back in under its own weight, well lubricated by the heavy flow of pre-cum.

Jay threw his head back again and groaned, his entire body visibly shuddering.

Sean pulled it slowly out, through that last bend, driving Jay into wracking shudders. He released it and let it glide back down until it stopped at the deep bend, then he turned it and let it slide fully in again. Jay nearly convulsed. Sean pulled it out a couple of inches again, until it was in the middle of that bend, held it there, and rotated it. Jay groaned again as his body shuddered. Sean released it, but the wand remained stationary. Jay was panting. The goosebumps were gone, but sweat broke out all over his body. Every muscle shuddered so powerfully that he couldn't talk when Sean asked how he liked it. All he could manage was a weak grunt.

"Nod if you want me to keep going," Sean told him.

Jay nodded vigorously, mostly by letting his shuddering muscles do the work.

Sean's fingers felt the little bead deep in Jay's cock, stuck in that last bending just within the beginning of his sack. He felt the bead slide as he moved the rod up and down, slowly, twisting and turning it. Jay panted heavily and muscles all over his body twitched and shivered.

Sean pulled the wand gently upward, feeling the bead moving inside the thick tube. He loved feeling its movement behind the skin of Jay's cock. He continued pulling more and more of the wand out of Jay each time he pulled upward. A large wash of clear pre-cum with little swirls of white rushed out each time Sean pulled the rod upward further than before. The fluids ran down the underside of Jay's cock and around Sean's fingers as they probed and followed the bead's progress.

Jay was lost in ecstasy. It was an order of a magnitude more intense and satisfying than anything before. His body began rocketing toward climax. He tried to tell them, but all he could do was grunt faintly in time with the movements of the rod inside of his urethra.

His anus clenched, his balls ached, his hips begged to thrust. It was all he could do to hold them still. His cock pulsed powerfully, and Sean began pulling the instrument out of Jay, knowing what was about to happen. With the last inch still inside, Sean let it slide back in an inch, against that first bend, then tapped the side of the wand.

Jay growled from deep in his throat at every slight movement of the wand, but the sensations as Sean tapped the wand exploded across his body. He was beyond speech and even thought. The sensations inside his cock, racing deeply into the base of it and through to his ass and his spine wracked his body.

Sean pulled nearly all of the wand out, causing more mixed clear and white fluids to run out and down across his fingers. He began turning it as he dipped it in deeper and pulled it nearly out, pushing and pulling the bead through the first bending, his fingers closely following the movements. He felt Jay's cock swell fully, and pulse, and Jay's breath break. He saw the flex run through Jay's entire cock. He let the wand slip as far as it could, back past the first bend down to the second, where it slowed and stopped. Then he spun it as he pulled it upward.

Jay screamed. Paul reacted and reached for Sean's hand. Billy grabbed him in a bear-hug.

"Just wait," Billy said firmly. "He's just blowing his wad."

Paul watched closely for any sign that Jay was in pain, and

wasn't sure that Billy was right. He wondered if he could break Billy's hold if Jay screamed like that again. But Jay's next scream was obviously one that wasn't from severe pain. It was guttural and nearly hoarse, and his shuddering body convulsed. Sean pulled the rod upward and bobbed it up and down inside the very end of Jay's cock, holding his cock still with his other hand. The thick, long cock warped and bent and twisted.

Sean pulled the rod out of Jay's cock and a large amount of clear fluid welled up and out and began running down the underside of Jay's long, thick cock. Sean pulled the skin of Jay's cock back tight to the base, sending deep flexing ripples through it. Paul watched, amazed, as pre-cum began flowing out of the reddened hole in an amount that was astounding.

Sean said loudly, "Thrust your hips, Jay! Fuck my fist!"

Jay thrust upward once and screamed again, then stopped moving, his breathing stopped as well. Sean stroked his cock once, then paused, then again. Then a large, thick, white streamer shot high into the air, above all of their heads. Jay screamed. Sean pulled the skin of Jay's cock back tight and held it there firmly. Before the first huge wad fell onto the bed, another fired upward, twisting and twirling. Another arced high before the second one landed. Another. Another.

Jay's body convulsed in time now with the shots of semen. Not that he meant to, it was instinct. He was beyond thinking of doing so. He had barely heard Sean's shouted order to thrust, but then had fallen deep into a place where he was consumed by the most incredible sensations. He didn't know anything but his body's functions and the overwhelming pleasure. Pleasure so intense, it went beyond pain.

More cum launched from Jay's red hole. Another. Lower, but still huge and thick. Then suddenly more, in rapid succession, rising as high as Jay's mid-chest, landing there, firing so close together they almost seemed to be a constant stream, lower with each outburst, but so much of it. Jay's cock flexed with each ejaculation. Still more, but lower in speed and distance, leaving Jay's angry-looking head in a nearly steady stream. More, and more still, now nearly a spray and no longer thick streamers, barely pumping out, landing on his belly and spreading out, running down the underside of his heavy cock in thick, slow-moving streams of white.

Jay's entire body suddenly tensed and locked, then convulsed powerfully, as if he had been struck by someone. He howled in air and collapsed backward. His breaths rasped roughly, rapidly, worrying Paul. Sean let go of his cock, sliding his hand upward to capture as much of the hot, sticky semen as he could.

Billy let go of Paul, and he almost fell on top of Jay.

"Jay?" he asked, on his hands and knees, his face directly over Jay's deeply red and vacant face.

Jay didn't react at all. His eyes were half-closed, his breath loudly rushing in and out of him, his body shuddering, his chest heaving. He felt as if he'd never cum before in his life, and had just exploded with a ferocity that tore the insides of his gonads into shreds. The pressure and tension behind his scrotum were so heavy that he wondered if he could ever again have another orgasm. He was weak, shaky, drained. And completely satisfied.

"Jay?" Paul asked again, not as concerned now that he saw Jay's face form an enormous grin.

"H-h-u-u-h?" Jay groaned around the still quivering muscles of his body.

"Okay?" Paul asked gently.

"Fu-u-u-ck-king…" ragged breath, "b-e-e-etter…" panting breath, "t-t-than…" shivering intake of air, "o-o-o-kay."

More convulsions ran through his thin body, and Paul placed a hand on his chest. It was hot and sweaty, and slick with cum, and Jay's pounding heart hammered there, behind his heaving breaths.

"T-t-that… w-w-was… f-f-fucking… amaz-z-zing!"

Jay opened his eyes and saw Paul directly over him. Paul's dark eyes looked worried, and Jay could barely process that information. But once he did, he grinned wider and stretched up and kissed Paul deeply. Paul held Jay's head up with both of his hands and returned the kiss.

Jay's arms went around Paul's neck and he pulled himself up and Paul down.

"Great view from over here," Billy said to Sean, leaning onto his side with his face behind Paul's ass and slightly lower than his dark brown hole peeking through his cheeks. They were spread wide as Paul was on his knees with his arms under and around Jay on the bed, and his balls hung and

swayed with the motions of his passionate kisses with Jay.
"I bet!" Sean said, still licking his hand clean.

Chapter 7

Jay was breathing almost normally now, though small shudders still ran through his body at times as he continued kissing Paul. He'd never felt so wonderful.

"I didn't think it'd get him off. Just that alone." Sean said, after having licked his hand clean, and now cleaning the sounding rod with paper towel and rubbing alcohol.

"Two days without getting off," Billy said simply.

"He sure came enough," Sean said.

"And you didn't share, ass," Billy said.

Sean leaned over and kissed Billy deeply, sharing the flavor of Jay's semen.

"Fucking rocked ass," Jay said softly, shaking his head after he and Paul broke their lip-lock.

He could still feel small shudders in his muscles. It had been far beyond anything he could ever have dreamed up. His cock was sore and sensitive, and he had never known there were such sensitive nerves inside his urethra. They still sent signals to his brain, reminding him of their presence.

"He's very sensitive," Paul said, clearly meaning it in more ways than the obvious.

"Coming down?" Sean asked.

"Yeah," Jay breathed.

"Are you okay?" Paul asked.

"Oh, yeah!" Jay said, nodding quickly. "That was fuckin' amazing!"

"Your wad was fuckin' amazing!" Billy said appreciatively. "I never thought I'd see someone shoot like that."

Jay laughed in embarrassment, his partially engorged cock wobbling over his balls between his still spread thighs.

Sean drew up his legs and kneeled over Jay's almost smoking groin. He gently grasped the still fat and shiny cock and held it upright.

Jay groaned a long, deep, shaking, "Aw-w-w-w," at the touch and movement.

"Going to be really touchy for a while," Sean said.

"Wait 'till ya take a piss!" Billy laughed.

Sean said, "Paul, why don't you clean up his chest. Tickle and lick his nipples while you're at it. And Billy can get his belly."

Paul grinned embarrassedly, and hesitantly began after sharing a red-faced grin with Jay. Jay covered his eyes with his arm and bit his lower lip. Sean held the heavy cock upright and began licking clean the soft, pale skin around the base and the sandy bush, then moved on to his balls. Billy licked his belly and chest clean.

The tickling sensations were awesome. He giggled and writhed, unable to stand the massive overload of sensations that three mouths and six hands provided on his already tingling body.

He nearly flinched each time Paul touched one of his sensitive nipples, and any movement of his cock by Sean made him shudder. The inside of it still sent tingling sensations to his brain by rippling up through his balls, prostate, ass, and spine.

"Awww, Gawd!" he droned slowly and repeatedly, his breath speeding up again.

After a few minutes of the three boys licking, kissing, and tickling him, his cock was throbbingly hard and the first drop of pre-cum glistened at the dark red hole in the tip. The head was dark red as well, nearly purple. Sean still held it softly, never having moved it an inch, and not providing even one stroke.

"All clean?" Sean asked.

"Yup," from Billy and, "Yes," from Paul.

Paul still ran his hand over Jay's chest and looked into Jay's brown eyes with his own nearly black ones. They grinned at each other, giggling.

"Okay, hands off," Sean said, then reached into the little overnight bag.

He held up two pairs of handcuffs, then handed them to

Paul.

"One on his wrists, one on his ankles. Not too tight."

Paul moved to comply, laughing softly with Jay. Sean removed the black rubber tie-down straps and handed them to Billy. Once Paul had Jay's wrists and ankles cuffed, Billy connected the cuffs to the headboard and footboard on the far side of the bed. This stretched Paul out flat, near the wall.

It was an incredible sight to all three, but Paul nearly came as he soaked in Jay's naked, glistening body. He didn't know why he was so attracted to nerdy guys, or Jay in particular, but he was, and he knew it. Jay's long, lean, slim body, his curly blond hair, fair brows, deep brown eyes, pale skin, small, hard, pink nipples, and large, thick cock with its bushy blond pubes drove him crazy.

He thought the two buff jocks were hot, too, just not as much as Jay.

Sean's dark-green eyes stood out against his pale complexion. His dark-brown hair was neat and smooth. He was slightly muscular, and well-developed, but nearly lean. And hung. It was nearly as long as Jay's, something around seven inches, but wasn't nearly as thick. It wasn't straight, either, but curved a little to the left. The hair at the base was so dark a brown it was nearly black. The head was prominent and heavily ridged, and with a large, oval, open hole in the tip. And was now darkly red and moist with large amounts of pre-cum. His balls hung low and were large, and dark hair showed clearly on the white skin of it and onto his thighs.

Billy was even stronger and buffer than Sean. His red hair turned Paul on, especially his brightly red patch at the base of his six-inch, pink cock. His gray eyes, freckles, and pale complexion also attracted Paul's taste. Billy's balls hung low and were fairly large. The head of his cock was smooth, rounded, almost pointed, and furiously pinkish-red now, as pre-cum oozed out it.

"Enjoying the sights?" Sean asked.

Paul snapped his eyes upward and saw that both of them were watching him, smiling. He blushed furiously and tried not to grin.

"Great view from here, too," Billy said again, laughing.

Sean and Billy both liked Paul's compact and powerful frame. His body was hard from weight lifting and exercises, and wrestling every day. His short, black, straight hair and his black eyes in his round, brown face gave him a nearly Hispanic or American-Indian appearance. Both boys wondered if either or both were in Paul's heritage. The thick black bush that his six inches of sturdy, textbook cock protruded from matched the hair on his chest between his large, brown nipples. His balls were smallish and didn't hang far from his body. The darker skin on his scrotum couldn't hide the black hair that sprouted there thickly and spread to his powerful thighs and legs.

"Ready for your turn?" Sean asked him.

"Uh, I'm not so sure I want to," Paul said hesitantly.

"Don't have to, but you don't know what you're missing," Sean said.

Paul looked to Jay, who nodded furiously, and said, "You got to, Paul!"

"You're on quiet time from now on," Sean said, then nodded at Billy.

Billy reached over and wrapped his fingers around Jay's balls with a leering grin. Jay hissed his breath inward with a grimacing grin. The threat of the pain fired all of his nerves and swelled his semi-erect penis.

"What if I don't like it?" Paul asked.

"Then we stop. But you saw Jay," Sean said, grinning. "I doubt you'll cum from it. Jay hasn't gotten off since Thursday night."

Paul looked to Jay questioningly, who nodded.

"It's really weird and kinda painful, but you gotta stick with it," Billy advised.

Paul looked to Jay again, and Jay nodded vigorously with a huge grin.

Paul grinned and nodded at Sean.

"Excellent! Sit like we did earlier, and we'll get started!"

Paul sat with his legs widely apart, and Sean moved to sit the same way, facing him, his knees over Paul's. Billy placed the antiseptic, lubricant, and the urethral sounds near Sean, then re-grasped Jay's balls.

Paul still wasn't sure he was going to let this happen, but Jay had loved it, clearly, and the desire to be at least as daring and brave as Jay was powerful. He leaned back onto his hands, as Jay had done, as Sean squeezed his head and licked away the pre-cum that rolled out. His body was tingling powerfully, and the long sexual thrill of the foreplay, then sucking Billy's cock, and then watching Sean bring Jay to such an incredible climax had built up an enormous pressure already. Paul wasn't sure how long he would last once any real pleasure was given him. He wondered briefly if he would cum from the stimulation of the probe, but sincerely doubted it.

"This is gonna feel weird," Sean said, then grasped Paul's rock hard and bouncing cock and placed the tip of the tube near the opening of his penis.

It was the first time someone else had touched him. He shuddered all over. His cock was so hard it almost hurt. He tingled from the base of his cock, up through his balls, through his anus, and up his spine. His breathing was fast and shallow.

Sean gently slid the tip of the antiseptic tube into the small hole of Paul's penis, making Paul's cock throb and dance. Paul held back a grunt at the unfamiliar sensation. Then the feeling of the cool, tingling fluid entering his urethra caused his thighs to tense and a small, high sigh to escape. Paul panted for several breaths as the first real stimulation to his organ by someone else raced through his body.

Sean removed the tip of the tube and kept the end of Paul's cock pinched closed, then once he had put the tube down, he began massaging the lubricant down Paul's urethra with his fingers.

"Fuck," Paul hissed.

"Weird, huh?" Sean asked with a grin.

Paul nodded. The sensation was the strangest thing he had ever felt. It was like toothpaste felt in his mouth; tingly and sparkly. As Sean's fingers worked the lubricant deeper, his breath increased and his body tensed. He felt his balls rising and his sack tightening.

"Wow," he said softly.

"Nice?" Sean asked.

Paul nodded, grinning.

Sean's fingers continued massaging Paul's urethra, moving down his six inches and then continuing to follow the tube behind Paul's tight sack. Paul's balls were tightly constrained and it required careful work to follow the tube between and above them. Paul shivered a little as Sean's fingers moved along his tube until it vanished deep inside of him. Sean massaged the hard organ there, sending strong shivers through Paul's legs and back. A large drop of pre-cum appeared at the hole, thick and shiny, mixed with lubricant.

"So weird!" Paul sighed loudly.

"Like it?" Sean asked.

"Sorta, I guess."

"You're hard as an iron rod, so you don't not like it," Sean answered, grinning.

Paul snickered.

"How is it?" Jay asked.

"It's fucking weird!" Paul said, a grin on his dark-red lips.

The cool tingling was an entirely new sensation, and Paul wasn't sure if he liked it or not. It wasn't unpleasant, but it was so odd. His cock sure didn't mind, as it was as hard as it had ever been.

Sean put down the tube of antiseptic, then picked up the smallest of the rods and applied a drop of lubricant to the small, oval tip.

"This will feel weird. But bear with it. It can end up the most incredible thing you've ever felt. Relax, don't move, and let me know if it hurts. Okay?" Sean said, holding Paul's dark eyes with his own.

Paul put on a firm face and nodded at Sean.

Sean continued holding Paul's eyes, and firmly stated, "Remember, don't move, and let me know if it hurts. Okay?"

Paul nodded again, not as sure as he put on. He was scared. He didn't get scared often or easily, but he was now. Having someone touch his naked body and his erection for the first time was quite a lot of excitement, but having to put himself into someone's hands in such a way was a huge thing for him. The steel rod looked to be ten feet long and sharp as a spike as Sean held it above the tight hole at the end of his throbbing erection.

Paul leaned forward.

"Don't do that when I've got the spike in," Sean said. "You won't like that."

"This is fucking weird!" Paul complained, and grabbed Sean's hand that held the rod.

Billy advised, "If you don't let go of Sean, I'll give Jay's balls a real squeeze."

"You do and I'll come over there and-"

"Just take it, Paul. I loved it! Try it!" Jay said, cutting him off.

Jay winced as Billy applied pressure to his balls.

"Damn it!" Paul said angrily.

"It's okay!" Jay said quickly.

Billy didn't apply pressure again, but gave Jay a warning look.

"Back off a second?" Jay said questioningly to Billy. "Let me talk?"

Billy looked to Sean, who nodded, still holding the rod against Paul's hole.

"Paul, don't worry if they hurt me. I'm not really being hurt. Okay? It's part of the fun. They won't really hurt me. Just making it fun. Relax. Enjoy it. It's fun. Okay?"

Paul visibly relaxed a little, then nodded.

"But if you really hurt him, you'll fucking regret it," Paul said to Billy.

"If I really hurt him, I'll regret it because I did, not because of what you might try to do to me. Okay?" Billy said firmly. "I like Jay, he's a great guy. I'll only hurt him enough so he's scared. It might really hurt him, but that's what he likes. So relax, get into it, and let yourself have some fun. Unwind, damn."

"I know you don't have any reason to trust us, not yet, anyway, but try to. Jay does. What does that tell you?" Sean asked.

Paul shrugged.

"This isn't a competitive sport. It's a cooperative one. We give each other what the other wants. Jay wants to worry he might be hurt, so he has to be hurt sometimes to make it a real threat. He gets off on it. We don't hurt him to hurt him. We hurt him rarely, but hurt him a tiny bit a lot. He gets off on it. If you don't, fine, but let him have what he likes. I'll try to give you what you like. But if Jay likes the threat of pain, he has to know the pain can really come, or else it's a hollow threat and he don't enjoy it. Okay?"

"Is that true?" Paul asked Jay.

Jay nodded so vigorously, Paul no longer had any doubts. Paul nodded.

"So don't worry if Billy hurts Jay some. Jay wants it, or he'd tell us no to. And he wouldn't talk during quiet time.

Right, Jay?'

Jay nodded vigorously, then said, "I like some pain, just the, being scared of it, it's such a turn on! Ouch! Damn it! Yeah!"

Billy had squeezed and tugged Jay's balls, and now grinned at Jay, then Paul.

"I knew that was coming, Paul. See? Ouch!"

Billy and Jay giggled.

Paul grinned, then looked at Sean and nodded.

"Okay," Sean said with a nod. "This is gonna feel weird."

"Fuck," Paul whispered, not believing he was going to let Sean insert anything into his dick, let alone a metal rod.

Sean held onto Paul's cock so that his fingertips were along the small tube beneath it, then positioned the tip of the wand against his small, closed hole. He rotated the wand, spreading the thick mixture of pre-cum and lubricant there. The cold metal against the sensitive tip sent shivers up Paul's cock.

"Oh, my God," Paul nearly whispered.

"Remember, stay still. Move and it can hurt like hell. If it gets really painful, say so, otherwise bear it like a man," Sean said directly into Paul's face.

Paul nodded.

"Here goes," Sean said, and began twisting the rod as he applied a small amount of pressure.

The little bud pushed the tip of Paul's cock inward, then suddenly the hole spread open and the metal tip popped inside. Paul shuddered and bit off a gasp. His cock jumped, and the movement made the little bead send shocks of both pleasure and pain through him.

"Oh, shit," Paul gasped, almost reaching for Sean's hand. "Stop it."

"Does it hurt?" Sean asked, looking at Paul's face, judging.

"Yes. No. Sort of. I don't think I like it," Paul said quickly.

"If you can get past that, it'll feel really good," Sean advised.

"I did it," Jay said, flinching as Billy applied pressure to his nuts.

"Take the pain like the burn when you're lifting weights," Billy said. "Make it yours. Own it."

Paul nodded. He understood exactly what Billy meant. He intended to take the entire thing, if it fit, so long as it didn't hurt too much. He stared down at the rod poking into his penis. It was a bizarre sight, and he couldn't believe he was allowing it to happen. But the mixture of pain and pleasure was alluring and very different, and very exciting. His whole body was alive with exquisite shivering tension.

Sean's fingertips followed the little bead as it slid in nearly an inch, then slowed and stopped. Paul's cock twitched in his hand.

"First bend," Sean said. "Okay?"

"Fucking bizarre!" Paul replied.

The thing caused the sensitive nerves inside of his cock to fire up, forcing intense waves of pulsing pleasure and pain to roll through it.

Sean twisted the wand, and Paul shivered. Sean let his finger rest on the end of it. It began sliding downward again. Paul shuddered and gasped. The small thing was creating sensations far too big for its size. It felt as if it were far larger. The wild tingling ran deeply through his cock and ass and up his spine, clear to the base of his skull, where it spread through his brain like sparkling fireworks. His head went back on his neck and he groaned deep in his chest. His feet turned inward as he fought the urge to move his hips.

Jay knew what he was feeling, and watching it happen was incredibly erotic. His own cock was hard, throbbing, and leaking pre-cum onto his belly above his navel. Billy had released his balls, and without even that input, his body screamed for any touch at all.

Sean let the rod rest two inches into Paul's cock and watched Paul's body tremble. Tiny wakes of movement ran through Paul's thick thighs. He could feel the little bead as it rested just two inches into Paul's pulsing cock. The head was nearly purple, and his balls were tight against his body.

"How is it?" Sean asked.

"Man. Like Jay said. Tiny little hurts, but so many, and they all add up to fucking awesome!"

"Going to help it a bit. Gonna multiply now, not just add!"

"Oh, fuck."

Paul shuddered in anticipation. It wasn't like he had thought, and was far better than he had. The thing caused such powerful sensations. It was like the first time he had discovered masturbation raised to the power of ten.

Sean turned the wand, and Paul gasped loudly, more shudders wracking his body. Even his shoulders shook. As the wand began sliding deeper again, Paul groaned at the intensity of it. His shoulders visibly shook, so much that even Jay could see their movement.

Paul's cock pulsed and throbbed, and each time, the wand slid deeper. Sean followed the bead as it slid past the front fold of Paul's scrotum, and moved his fingers so that he could follow its progress deeper. Paul shook from knees to shoulders, shuddering and shivering.

"Jesus Christ! It's fucking awesome!" Paul nearly shouted.

He ached to thrust his hips, to take more of the device in deeply, but Sean's warning rang in his head. It was all he could do to keep from forcing his hips up and off the bed. He was panting and staring at the ceiling, mouth open.

Sean allowed the rod to slide the rest of the way, until it stopped. He let it rest there for a few moments, knowing it was bottomed out. Then he scraped his fingernail over the rough side of the handle.

"Shit!" Paul said loudly.

Tremors ran along his arms and shoulders, even his pectoral muscles across his chest. His breath vibrated with those tremors, they were so deep and powerful. He had never felt anything like it.

"Have a look, it's bottomed out," Sean said.

Paul looked down to see two or three inches of the metal rod sticking out of the hole of his cock. He was stunned. The sight made even more waves of pleasure wash through him and made his cock bounce. That sent even more waves of pleasure through him.

"Oh-h-h-h, man!" he sighed, amazed.

Sean gently gripped the flat handle and turned it. Paul shuddered as powerfully as he had so far and grunted. Sean pulled the wand upward just an inch, then let it slide down again. Up, then down, again and again.

Paul nearly screamed, "Fuck! Oh, fuck!"

"Is it going to finish you off?" Billy asked in awe.

"Oh, God! I think so! Fuck!"

The most intense waves of pleasure he had ever felt rushed through him, mixing with the strange near-pain, making all of his muscles contract and relax in pulses out of his control. He was helpless to stop them, and that was another new sensation to him. He was used to having complete control over his body, but now he had nearly none.

Jay shivered as he watched. His body thrummed, aching for any touch at all, anything, even a soft breath across his skin.

Billy watched, engrossed, his red cock bouncing and dripping.

Sean pulled the wand upward until he felt the resistance of the deepest bend, and then he bobbed it up and down there.

"Shit! Fuck! Damn!" Paul blurted. "I'm gonna fuckin' cum!"

Sean pulled the wand upward, and clear fluid mixed with white flowed out of the tight hole around the metal rod. He felt Paul's cock swell and thrust upward. He pulled the rod out as quickly as he dared.

Paul's breath caught, stopped, and his body tensed and held.

As the rod exited, a large flow of mixed clear and white fluids preceding it, Paul's cock swelled and throbbed powerfully, then Sean felt the heavy flow of semen through Paul's urethra near his sack as his prostate pumped.

Sean saw a white blur and felt something strike his cheek and nose. He laughed as more fired from Paul's cock, most of it hitting him in the face.

Paul twisted and gasped as he felt the most powerful orgasm of his life squirt from him with a pressure he didn't know his body could create. He grunted, "Fuck," as he fired onto Sean's face. He'd never cum with someone else before, but to see his own semen splashing onto Sean's face was too much. He was sure it prolonged and intensified his orgasm. His cock felt as if burning coals were being pushed up through it. The next shot joined the first on Sean's face, as did the third and fourth. The next shots landed in descending height from Sean's neck to his belly, nearly coating his front with semen.

"Six," Billy counted, "Seven. Eight. Nine. I guess ten, no, eleven. Wow. The rest are just leftovers being squeezed out, but I'd still say an even dozen was fair. And four all over Sean's face. Fuckin' hot!"

"Awww, shit!" Paul exclaimed and fell onto his back across Jay's legs, panting rapidly.

Billy crawled to Sean and began kissing and licking his face clean.

Jay nearly groaned, his body demanding release, or at least some kind of sensation. Paul's warm shoulders and head on his shins were merely an agonizing tease. He stretched his legs, popping his knee and hip joints. It was the only thing he could do to stave off the tension. It was driving him crazy, watching, but not taking part. And he had to pee very badly.

The sight of Paul's ecstatic face as he recovered was hot, and Jay wanted nothing more than to rush over and lick and suck his cock clean. But he couldn't move. Paul's deeply purple cock quivered and dripped a white string onto his tan skin, shrinking into the black bush, pulling the sting longer and longer. Jay drooled at the sight.

Paul turned his head to look up Jay's legs to his face. Jay grinned happily at him.

"You were right. Man, fuckin' Aiy!"

Jay nodded quickly, remembering to remain quiet. Paul slid up his legs, brushing Jay's swollen cock with his lips far too briefly, then up his belly, chest, and finally kissing him deeply.

"Hey, hey, none of that," Sean said firmly, Billy now cleaning his chest and belly.

Paul stopped kissing Jay, but only after another long, slow one. He sat up and shivered violently.

"Fuck."

"Guess you're sensitive, too," Billy said with a grin.

Paul laughed and turned a little redder.

"I think it was just that he's never had anything happen but jacking himself off," Sean said.

"Well, sure beats jacking off, that's for sure," Billy said. "How about it, Paul? How'd you like it?"

"That was…"

"The best thing since your first jack-off?" Billy asked.

"Hell yes!" Paul agreed with a laugh.

"Just wait until you have to piss, though," Billy laughed. "Won't be so much fun, I think. But I love it."

Jay shook his arms and legs against the cuffs, rattling them loudly.

"I guess Jay's about to find out," Sean laughed.

Chapter 8

Billy released Jay from the cuffs and led him to the bathroom.

After watching the two naked boys walk out of the room, Sean bounced his eyebrows at Paul.

"What?" Paul asked suspiciously.

"Trust me yet?"

"Well, maybe. Some. Why?"

Sean leaned over the edge of the bed and held up two sets of handcuffs, grinning.

"I don't know," Paul said doubtfully. "Once you get them on…"

"I know. If you're not ready, fine. There's other things to do."

"More? I don't think I can get hard again."

"Owww," came from the bathroom, then Jay's laughter. "Owww," again, and more laughter. Billy's laughter, too. "Oh, geeze! Owww!" Jay laughed. The sound of urine into the toilet came, then stopped as Jay groaned another, "Owww!"

Sean laughed. Paul looked a little worried, but grinned as well, then asked, "Does it really hurt?"

"Really? No. Stings a lot, though."

"Owww!" and another short shot of urine into the toilet. More short runs of urine and more soft, laughing complaints from Jay. Finally, a long, steady stream, and Jay moaned, "Ahhh," in satisfaction.

Sean and Paul were grinning as Billy dragged Jay back into the bedroom. Jay grinned ear to ear and was blushing more than slightly. His long cock was still more than soft, but far from hard.

"Bad?" Paul asked.

Jay shook his head, still grinning, and turning redder.

"Hope not. I got to go," Paul said.

"So go," Sean said. "But I've got to see this."

"You want to watch?" Paul asked.

"Sure do. This can be entertaining."

"Me, too," Billy said.

Jay rattled his cuffs.

"In front of all of you?"

"If you're up to it," Sean said with a snicker.

"Geeze. Well, I got to go."

They followed him and stood around him as he aimed his soft dick.

"Ow! Damn it!"

The three giggled.

"Ouch!"

They all laughed.

"Oh, man! Bitch!" Paul groaned.

A small, short squirt.

"Fuck."

Another short squirt.

"Damn!" Paul laughed.

Another squirt and another expletive. Longer streams, more cusses.

"Oh, this is fucking ridiculous!" Paul complained, laughing.

Finally, Paul managed to maintain a steady stream.

"Ohhh, man," he groaned. "That's really wild."

"Drives ya crazy, huh?" Sean asked, then slapped his ass once he'd finished urinating, firmly, but not hard.

"This has been one unforgettable afternoon," Paul said, grinning.

"Not over yet. Lots more to come," Sean said with bouncing eyebrows.

"I won't get hard for hours," Paul said.

"Oh, I bet you're hard and drooling in the next half hour," Sean said.

"How? I came so hard, it hurt."

"Well, you're going to work a spike in me, then you're gonna do Billy."

"Oh, man," Paul groaned.

"He likes Billy's red pubes," Jay said, then presented his

balls for Billy's punishment with a cute, almost shy grin.

Billy reached out, cupped them, then squeezed, hard and harder, until Jay winced. Then he squeezed just a little harder before he let them go, making Jay squeak. Jay's large cock began throbbing upward.

Sean and Billy, while never going completely soft, began enlarging as well. Paul was surprised to feel his own sore cock growing.

"You ever done anything but plain-jane jerking it?" Sean asked Paul as they returned to the bedroom.

Paul looked confused at the question, and watched as Billy placed Jay back on the edge of the bed near the wall and connected the black rubber straps to the chains of the handcuffs on his wrists and ankles.

"You really like that, huh?" Paul asked Jay.

Jay nodded, grinning wider, and blushing again.

The other three boys sat on the bed, and Sean motioned Paul to come close to Jay's prone body, along with himself and Billy.

"Might as well play with it while it's laying here," Sean said, reaching out to touch and caress Jay's body. "Just stay away from his dick and balls. Just play with his skin and make him crazy."

Jay whimpered, mostly in expectation, and bit down on his lower lip with all of his upper teeth as six hands began roaming across his body. The sensual sensations lit up his nerves, and his slightly sore cock began reaching full mast.

They continued to caress him as they talked.

"So, you just jack it?" Sean asked Paul.

Paul blushed further and shrugged.

"Ever stopped before you shot, then started again?"

Paul shook his head.

"Ever stuck a finger up your ass?"

Paul shook his head.

"How about at least massaged your prostate from outside?"

Paul shook his head, looking confused.

"That place I rubbed when I was pushing the lube in? Up under your balls? Made you jerk and shake?"

"Oh. I know what the prostate is, I didn't know it felt…"

"Great to play with?" Billy asked.

Paul grinned and nodded.

"You at least play with your nuts while you jack off?"

Paul nodded, very red-faced, grinning shyly. He wasn't used to talking to someone about such things. And especially not with three other boys, all naked and hard, and one restrained as they all touched and tickled him. And it was Jay, at that. His heart raced at the realization of what he was doing, and with whom. His cock jerked, now fully hard again, and growing dark at the head. He looked down at his erection, surprised it was back so soon, and marveling at the tingling, tickling, prickling sensations the inside still sent to his brain. He found it completely unbelievable that he had taken a metal rod inside of it, and that Sean had moved it around inside of him, creating the most intense and incredible sensations of his life, until he had cum harder and more than he ever had before.

"Ever tried a little pain?" Sean asked. "You know, pinch your nipples while you jerk?"

Paul shook his head and looked up and away from his tingling erection.

"This dude is totally vanilla," Billy said almost unbelievingly.

"Ever tried sucking your own?" Sean asked next.

Paul shook his head, looking completely disbelieving.

"Maybe you have to be long, like you," Billy said. "We regular guys just can't."

Paul looked confused, then asked Sean, "You actually can?"

Sean nodded.

"No way," Paul said doubtfully.

Sean grinned, turned a little sideways, checked behind himself, then rolled so that his legs went over and behind his head until his knees were on the bed, putting his ass high in the air. Paul blinked, stunned, as Sean pulled his ass with his hands and stretched his neck up, and the head of his long cock slipped through his lips.

"Holy hell," Paul whispered in awe. "If I could do that, I'd never leave my bedroom!"

Everyone laughed, including Sean, who had to un-tuck a bit to do so. Paul looked at Jay, curiosity obvious. Jay snickered, turned red, then nodded.

"Really?" Billy asked.

Jay nodded more firmly.

"Wanna see?" Sean asked Billy and Paul.

Both nodded, and Sean unrolled. Billy freed the rubber strap from the cuffs on Jay's ankles, and Jay promptly rolled his legs up until his knees were beside his ears and began sucking in his own cock, until the head's edges vanished. It wasn't as good as someone else doing it to him, as he had learned during the previous week, but it was suction and lips and tongue on his aching, needing cock, and his body exploded with the pleasure.

"Holy fucking shit," Paul said admiringly. "That's the hottest thing I've ever seen!"

"He's hot. I love his ass," Billy said, then stuck a finger in his mouth and then quickly into Jay's upraised, exposed hole.

Jay shuddered visibly and groaned around his own cock in his mouth. Billy stuck the finger in deeply, rotated it, and pressed against the hard organ inside. Jay grunted loudly and all three boys saw his body shuddering.

"That's enough," Sean said.

Billy removed his finger, then had to pull Jay's legs down to stop him from sucking himself further. Jay was obviously let down.

"Roll him back up," Sean said, then said to Paul, "Keep his cock out of his mouth. I want to try something. And don't stroke it."

Paul blinked, then with a grin, he held Jay's long cock away from his mouth. Jay grinned and laughed at Paul, who giggled back. Sean moved so that he was directly behind Jay's back and ass, then licked from the small of Jay's back, through his crack and over his hole, then up and over his sack. Then he went back down, tongue trailing the way. Jay squeaked repeatedly. Sean's trips got shorter and shorter, and soon, he was concentrating on Jay's tan and brown hole with his tongue.

Jay was panting and whimpering, and Paul felt Jay's cock warping and twisting with nearly every movement of Sean's tongue. He had heard of analingus, but had never given it much thought. But watching Sean's pink tongue probe and lick Jay's hole made Paul's cock throb and ache, and drip. In fact, his whole body was trembling with the sight.

Sean put his lips tightly around Jay's hole and pushed saliva inside it. Jay quivered and whimpered. Then he slid two fingers in at the same time. Jay shuddered, barely holding back the groans of intense pleasure. Sean pushed the fingers in all the way, then turned them and found Jay's prostate.

"Awww, fuck!" Jay cried out as Sean massaged.

Sean withdrew his fingers and grinned as he said, "That's that for now," and slapped Jay's exposed, taut ass cheeks hard enough to turn them red and make Jay flinch strongly. "Tie him back down."

Jay groaned sadly, like a kid who'd just been told he couldn't play with his new toy.

"Don't worry, you guys can do whatever you want with each other when we're not around. Unless you want to be my bitches and I tell you not to touch each other unless I'm here."

Paul didn't seem too enthusiastic about that idea.

"Yeah, you're not gonna be anyone's bitch, are ya?" he asked Paul.

"I don't think so," he said firmly.

"But you might make a good master for Jay," Sean said thoughtfully. "You like wrestling your opponent down? Having the power?"

Paul nodded, blushing, understanding where Sean was leading.

"I like owning him, yeah. I like knowing I can bend him into a fucking pretzel and there ain't nothing he can do about it but take it."

"Oooh, daddy," Billy crooned. "I told ya, Sean, he'd be a good master."

"Do ya think you can make Jay go all day without letting him get off? Play with him, fuck his ass, make him suck you, lick your ass, fuck you, suck him, but not let him cum all day?"

Oh, God! Jay thought with such glee he thought his heart might rupture! Please! Let Sean and Billy just be the opening act! Please, Paul! Make me do whatever you want! Make me yours! Be my master! Own me! Please!

Jay's thoughts were clear on his face, his expression. Paul couldn't miss it. And the idea raced through Paul like wildfire. The thought of controlling and pleasing Jay at the same time, of making him wait all day, driving him insane with desire and pleasure, drove him insane with the desire to do so.

Paul grinned hugely and nodded.

"Billy, cuff yourself," Sean said without looking away from Paul's face.

Billy dove off the bed and for the overnight bag, then rapidly applied the cuffs to his ankles then his wrists. He stood beside the bed, waiting, as Sean waved Paul to join him in the middle of the bed and then arranged the bag of sounding rods, antiseptic, tissues, and lube between them.

Sean looked at Billy then pointed at the bed. Billy sat down, then lay down. Sean reached over him, leaning down over the edge of the bed, his elbow in Billy's stomach, pulled two more black rubber straps out of his overnight bag, then pushed himself upright with the elbow in Billy's gut. Billy grunted loudly and smiled. Sean then connected the black straps to Billy's cuffs and the bed, stretching him out on the edge of the mattress.

Jay was now stretched out against the wall, Billy on the other side of the bed, and Paul and Sean sat between them, facing each other, the supplies between them.

"I don't want you skewering poor Jay here, so you're gonna practice on me and Billy. We ain't had any fun today yet, anyway. So, you remember some of what I said about how to use 'em? And how I did it?"

"Don't push, let it slide in. Don't force it. Don't let it touch anything before you use it. Use the antiseptic first, then lube inside, then the probe. And go slow. And ask if it's okay a lot."

Sean sat back on his arms, grinning, waiting, his long dick aimed almost at Paul's face.

Paul snickered, remembering where his own explosive orgasm had landed, and almost hoping that he managed to have Sean's do the same to him. He wrapped his fingers around Sean's long, thick cock, just behind the pronounced, out-turned edges of the purple head. Sean's head was heavy and blunt, with prominent edges and contours. It was noticeably wider than the slightly curved, nearly eight-inch shaft that aimed it to Sean's left.

"Is that metal rod thing gonna go around the curve? I mean, it's got that curve in it," Paul asked.

"It'll go. It bends a little, and my cock will straighten a bit, too. You have to make my dick go straight by holding it tight.

I'll show you how. Trust me. If it hurts, it'll be my fault, okay?"

Paul nodded, taking a glance at Jay lying next to him and Sean. Jay was watching closely, just able to see what Paul was doing to Sean's dick by sitting up as much as he could by pulling against the cuffs on his ankles. Jay grinned at him, making Paul grin back at him. Jay's longer, thicker cock lay on his belly, the thick tube prominent along its length. Paul couldn't wait to please and tease Jay, and the thought sent a ripple through his groin and down the length of his six inches.

"In time," Sean said playfully. "Now back to me. I'm fuckin' dyin' for it."

Paul turned back to Sean's eight curved inches and bulky head. The tube down the underside wasn't nearly as large and obvious as the one beneath Jay's. With the more than a slight curve along its length, Paul wasn't sure that the long metal rod would go easily or comfortably down it. But he knew Sean had taken it before and wanted it now.

Paul picked up the tube of lube and uncapped it.

"You need to insert the whole tip. My hole is open, like Jay's, so put the tip inside and hold it tightly closed, and squeeze some in, then work it down like I did to you. Let a little get on your finger or thumb, the one you're gonna work my tube with. Makes it easier if your finger is slick."

Paul followed the instructions and worked the lubricant down the length of Sean's long cock. He liked doing it. He liked holding Sean's cock, and rubbing his fingers down it, pushing the lube downward. It throbbed and swelled in his hand, and he liked that too. The heat, the softness over the hardness inside, the texture of the skin, and the contours of the curving length.

"Do me a solid, Paul," Sean said, taking the lube from him. He held Paul's hand, and ran a small bead of the lube along the inside of his thumb, across the webbing to his first finger, and along the side of that finger to the tip. "Make a ring, like an 'okay' sign. Right. Now, keep the finger and thumb touching all the time, and push it over the end of my dick and all the way down, then stroke me like that. End to base, all the way. Over and over. Don't let your finger and thumb open up any. Keep them tight as you go over my head, but never come apart. Make sure you rub the whole head both ways."

Paul looked a little confused but followed the instructions. The loop of his finger and thumb was too small to easily go over the thick, bulbous head, but he applied pressure and force. Sean gasped and shook a little as the tight loop deformed his head and pushed it back, then slid over it and down the curved shaft.

"Fuck, yes!" Sean groaned. "Like that. Over and over. Nice and slow."

The tight loop had to be forced over the head each time, going up and going down, and Sean gasped each time in both directions.

"Okay, stop!" Sean said quickly. "That can make me blow like that. Try it."

Paul did, and found that his smaller dick slid through easier, but it did feel incredible. He tightened the circle and it was even better.

"Nice, huh?"

"Yeah!" Paul answered, then looked at Jay.

"No. You're doing me right now. Billy next. He has to suffer and wait for now," Sean told him, handing him some paper towel. "Clean that up, and then put a little lube on the tip of the rod. Use the smallest one on the large side."

Paul removed the rod with the smallest bud at the tip from the side with all the largest sized ones. It was at least three times larger than the one Sean had used on Jay, and about four times as large as the one that Paul had endured. He knew it wouldn't go into his tiny hole without considerable discomfort at least, if not real pain. If at all.

Paul dropped a dollop of lubricant onto it and spun it, coating the entire little oval bud.

"Now hold it down, so the lube runs to the tip of the little bead, and put it at my hole."

Paul followed the directions, his hand beginning to shake as he placed the little bead at the entry to Sean's penis. The opening was darkly red, already wet with pre-cum, and open. The bead was larger than the opening.

"Hold my dick tight, take some of the curve out of it. Don't pinch off the tube, though. Right, like that. You catch on quick. Now, aim it straight down my cock. No angle. Don't let go, but let the weight of the spike pull it inside. Ohhh, man!'

Jay shuddered and moaned as he watched the rather large

oval disappear into Sean's hole. He could only imagine the intensity of the pleasure as the large thing entered and slid in deeper. His cock shuddered and more fluid increased the size of the pool of pre-cum inside his navel. He stretched himself out, popping a few joints, his body tingling with anticipation and empathetic sexual tension and pleasure.

Billy softly moaned and stretched out against the cuffs as well. He knew what that size felt like, and liked it, but he now preferred the larger ones, nearly the largest, even though his dick was much smaller than Sean's, and thinner, and his hole and urethra smaller as well.

Paul was entranced, watching and feeling what he was doing to Sean's large cock. He liked Sean's cock and his body, but he liked Billy's more, and he couldn't wait to touch and play with Billy's attractive, red-haired, pink cock next. But he really was looking forward to having Jay's long, thick cock in his hands.

But now, he had his hand full of Sean's big dick, and his other was busy following the wand as it slid slowly into the long thing. The dark head seemed to swallow it in turns as it pulsed and bobbed as the wand slid deeper. Sean's breathing sped up, and his thighs shuddered slightly.

"Doing really good, Paul. It's gonna slow down and stop here in a sec. My dick has that curve in it, so it needs some encouragement. Not like on you or Jay. More. But be gentle. Just let your finger lay on it, to add a little weight. That's all."

The probe slowed and stopped. Paul could feel where the little bud was, nearly halfway down the long cock. His own cock throbbed and released another drop of pre-cum. It rolled down his shaft, joining the rest along the top of his tight sack. He laid a finger on top of the flat handle. It didn't move. He looked up at Sean's face. He was grinning and red-faced, biting his lower lip.

"Twist, slow and careful, and let your finger push really easy," Sean advised him.

Paul did, and the wand slid in deeper. Sean gasped, and his cock pulsed thicker with each beat of his heart. His own cock jumped.

"Sooo, good," Sean groaned.

Jay's body trembled and his cock released more pre-cum into his belly-button. Watching Paul do that to Sean was possibly the hottest thing he had seen yet. Paul looked so absorbed, so careful. And Sean was obviously enjoying it a lot. The sight of Paul's cock leaking pre-cum down onto his balls made Jay's cock throb each time he looked there, away from what Paul's hands were doing to Sean's cock.

Billy's breathing was rapid, and his body warm with sexual energy. He loved doing that to Sean, and watching a new boy do it for his first time was very hot, aside from the fact that it was the sexy, buff, Paul. He couldn't wait for Paul to do it to him.

Sean was enjoying it immensely. The worry and fear that Paul would mess up added to it, but wasn't much of a real worry. Paul was careful and sure, and far from clumsy or awkward. And he followed Sean's instructions well. When the wand stalled again, due to the curve behind his cock, he told Paul to push gently.

Paul gave the wand a push and felt it slip in deeper. Sean's cock pulsed and throbbed with each beat of his heart. The long curve meant that the shaft of the rod was now pushing against the side of Sean's hole, noticeably, misshaping the hole quite a bit. He knew Sean was used to it, and liked it, or he would have him remove the thing, not tell him to apply more pressure.

Paul felt the resistance against the wand's further intrusion and wondered how much harder he should push against it. There was only an inch or so of shaft left outside of Sean's hole.

"That's it," Sean gasped. "Bottomed out. Fucking nice. Now, like we did to you and Jay, move it in and out. Twist it. Like giving head, you use your tongue and don't let me guess what's next. This, too. Okay?"

Paul moved it in and out of Sean's long cock, giving it twists and scraping his nail across the rough, flat edge from time to time.

"Think I can get you off with it?" Paul asked.

"No way, but go right ahead and try!" Sean answered.

Paul did. He moved the rod in and out, spun it, twirled it, allowed Sean's curve to return then straightened it again, moving the rod in various depths and ways. Sean began shivering, grinning widely.

"Think so still?" Paul asked.

"You're not gonna get me off that way. You can try all day. Go ahead. I won't mind a fucking bit!"

Billy laughed, which convinced Paul more than anything Sean had said. He nodded and began working the wand inside of Sean's cock. It was a huge turn on. He was in charge of Sean's pleasure, and he knew that he could hurt him if he wanted to. He didn't though. He wanted to make Sean cum, like he had done to him earlier. He wanted to work Sean's cock and drive him insane.

He experimentally loosened his grip on Sean's cock, allowing the curve to return. Sean gasped and shivered as the wand slid in and out, spun, and Paul rasped his thumbnail over the pebbled, textured side of the flat handle.

"Fuckin' Aiy! Nice touch!" Sean crooned. "You're a natural at this! Take it out."

Paul obeyed, and removed the rod, pushing pre-cum and lubricant out of the hole ahead of the bead.

"Wipe it clean with a tissue, then use the antiseptic on it, then put it back in the case," Sean said. Once that was done, Sean pulled the next-to-largest wand from the case and handed it to Paul. "Lube it, then put it in."

"You sure?" Paul asked.

"Do what I say," Sean said forcefully.

The bead on this wand was easily five times the size of the one Sean had used on him earlier, and he wasn't sure anyone could take it without pain. As he lubed it, he wondered if it would even go into Sean's hole. The hole in Sean's cock was open, an oval gap, but Paul was sure the bead was wider than it.

Sean's head was dark red, nearly purple, and the entire cock throbbed with his pulse. Paul grasped the long cock firmly, straightening the curve from it, then placed the bead against the hole. The device didn't go in, and Paul let his finger rest against it. He rotated it, but it still did not enter.

"Give it some encouragement," Sean said, leaning back onto his hands again, his body starting to shine with sweat.

Paul wiggled the wand, then pushed. The end of Sean's cock depressed around the hole, but the bead didn't go inside. He gently rotated it and pushed. Suddenly the bead was cocooned in the soft edges of the hole, and with only a slight touch, it slipped inside. Sean jerked and groaned deeply.

Tremors ran through his thighs as he fought to hold his hips still.

"Fu-u-u-u-ck," he laughed.

"Okay?" Paul asked.

"Fuck yes, okay!" Sean said.

Jay's body shuddered powerfully, and a loud whimper escaped. His body was crying for any sensation at all. Just a quick touch, anything. His cock had filled his navel with pre-cum, and more would overflow. His head was deep purple, and the entire length of his cock flexed periodically. His balls were so tightly against his body they hurt and were merely a slight hemispherical curve between his thighs.

Billy's pink six-inch cock had turned violet, and even the shaft had darkened. The small amount of foreskin was puffy and bunched behind his smallish, almost delicate, purple head. His pink scrotum was tight to his body.

Paul's short cock was dark as well. His head was nearly purple, and the hole red. It poked out of his dark bush, pointed upward, throbbing constantly.

Sean's long cock was dark and wet, dancing in Paul's grip. The first inch of the rod was inside of it now, and Paul could follow the progress of the huge bead with his eyes. Sean shuddered and grunted and told Paul to push.

"Won't it hurt?" Paul asked.

"Do what I tell you and don't ask questions," Sean ordered. "Just don't shove it, is all. Encourage it... firmly."

Paul obliged, twisting the rod as well. It didn't go easily, and he knew it was hurting Sean, but Sean liked it. Sean asked him to do it. Sean told him to do it.

"Fucking awesome!" Sean groaned. "Make it go. Not hard, just make it go!"

The large bead showed clearly, making a bulge in the thick tube as it passed the halfway point. The sight made Paul's cock twitch and bob. It was incredible. Paul felt his balls warm and that growing urge. A large wash of pre-cum oozed out as his cock swelled powerfully. The tingle inside was undeniable. He was sure it wouldn't take much at all for him to finish, and finish powerfully.

"Let it go," Sean ordered.

Paul did.

"Let go of my dick," Sean ordered.

Paul wasn't sure that was a good idea, but Sean told him to, so he did.

Sean's cock regained most of its curve, pushing against the straight rod. Sean groaned. More than half of the rod was inside him, and the bead was visible just past the halfway point. Sean shuddered, panting.

"You going to?" Paul asked.

"So close," Sean grunted, obviously trying to prevent it.

He shuddered for long moments, the sweat shining all over his body, his eyes tightly closed and grimacing. Finally, he shivered violently, then released a long, "Ahhh."

He opened his eyes and visibly relaxed.

"Close," he said softly, and grinned wider. "Now, go back to it."

Paul grinned and said, "I thought you said it wouldn't get you off?"

"Not that one. I never took this one before, though."

"Really?" Paul asked.

Sean nodded, then nodded at the wand sticking out of his hole.

Paul grasped it and twisted it, encouraging it deeper. It slid in. Sean shook and grunted. Paul encouraged it further.

"Shit, yeah!" Sean panted. "You're gettin' it! Like that!"

Sean began breathing harder and faster again, and his body broke out in a heavy sweat. He shuddered and grunted.

"Jack me. Like I showed you earlier."

Paul lubed the side of his first finger, the webbing between the finger and his thumb, and the inside of his thumb. Then he formed a tight circle and began forcing it up and down Sean's thick cock. Each time he forced his fingers over the prominent edges of Sean's head, Sean grunted and jerked, and his cock flexed along its entire length. Sean panted now, was covered with sweat, and his body was trembling almost constantly.

"God! Shit, yes! Fucking awesome!" Sean groaned around his rapid breaths.

All three other boys moaned softly in sympathy and their own pleasures.

"Ugh. Shit! Get it out! Not too fast! But get it out!"

"You goin' off?"

"Fuckin' hell I am!"

Paul felt Sean's cock throb and swell. He began pulling the

rod out, but not sure how fast he could without hurting him. Sean's hand grabbed his hand and he pulled.

"Don't stop jacking me! Fuck!"

The bead popped out, making a corresponding noise. Paul continued to stroke his tightly-circled finger and thumb along Sean's thick, long cock.

"Fucking cool!" Sean said happily as he thrust his hips forward and his cock through the circle of Paul's fingers.

Then cum flew from his cock, spraying out of it and splashing across Paul's belly. Sean jerked, moving his cock through the circle made by Paul's finger and thumb, and shot more hot semen onto Paul's abdomen. His eyes were tightly closed, his face red, as he fired another large wad, this one landing across Paul's thigh. Shot after shot of cum as Sean's cock throbbed in Paul's hand. More cum splashed onto Paul's cock, balls, and thighs.

"Nice!" Billy said, admiring the sight.

The noises of Paul's fingers squeezing Sean's cock as it was lubricated by the thick cum filled the room, accompanied by the soft groans of Jay.

Billy counted, "Four... five... six... seven... eight... oh man! Most he's shot in a while!"

Sean groaned wordlessly, his eyes tightly closed in a grimace of combined pain and ecstasy.

Jay groaned deeply, his entire body trembling as muscles rapidly clenched and released. His body threatened to ejaculate, but only threatened. It was near to it, and wanted to, but it lacked the stimulation.

Paul smiled and enjoyed the feeling of the hot semen landing on him and squishing between his hand and Sean's cock. It wasn't his face, but it was good enough. And the hot cum that landed on his own cock made it pulse and threaten to explode.

He watched the semen spray out of Sean. No thick ropes, no long strings, but rapid pulses of groups of beads and droplets. They spread out and covered a considerable area of his stomach, groin, and thighs. The smell was heavy in the air and made Paul's jaws ache. He kept stroking Sean's thick, long cock, paying attention to forcing his finger and thumb across the prominent edges of his head. Sean bucked and groaned each time.

For nearly a minute, Sean bore the near pain of it, then grabbed Paul's hand and removed it from his aching cock. Sean nearly collapsed onto his back with a loud whoosh.

"Man! Paul, you did fucking great!" Sean said once he had his breath slowed.

Paul saw Sean's large cock softening and drooping down over his balls, between his thighs. It made his cock twitch and his body tingle. He saw both Billy and Jay looking longingly at both Sean's sated body and his own erect, throbbing cock, and licking their lips. They were both nearly pulling their arms and legs off, yearning to join him in any way.

Paul used both hands to wipe and gather some of Sean's cum from his own cock and balls, then held each hand out so that Jay and Billy could barely reach his fingers. They licked and sucked his fingers energetically. Paul wiped more cum from Sean's cock, milking more from inside it, then held his fingers so that both boys had to stretch to the limits allowed by their restraints to lick his fingers.

Paul pulled his hands too far for either boy to reach and laughed. He wiped the last of the semen from himself and Sean, then teased both boys with his fingers as they stretched to the limit of their restraints before letting them have them.

"You're learning fast," Sean laughed.

Chapter 9

"Billy's gonna run out of pre-cum and get dehydrated if we don't get him off soon," Sean commented as he watched Billy and Jay stretch against their bonds to lick his cum from Paul's fingers.

"How long have you waited to get off before?" Paul asked.

"The longer, the better," Billy replied after cleaning Paul's fingers.

"He went all day for his birthday last month. Eleven times I got him close but stopped. Made him sweat like a fucking pig and shake like an earthquake. And when he came, it was the most I ever saw until Jay earlier. And it was so fucking' hot! Like steam!"

"And it huuuuurt!" Billy groaned. "I thought it wouldn't work ever again!"

"So, Paul, how about if you use the big sounder on him?"

"He can take that big one?" Paul asked, looking doubtful.

"Yup. Has. Usually work our way up, but I think today, we can just go right to it."

Billy blinked in surprise. He wasn't so sure he wanted the inexperienced Paul using the very largest on him, especially without one or two of the smaller ones first. But he knew Sean wouldn't have asked if he didn't think Paul had done well enough on himself first. Still, it was worrying, thus extremely exciting.

Paul saw the concern on Billy's face. He wasn't so sure he should jump right to the largest one either, but Sean seemed to know what he was doing. Paul looked at Sean for a moment and thought of asking him if he was sure, but Sean nodded and grinned.

"I know he can take it, and without smaller ones first. It'll just be really intense. You'll have to go slow and careful. Like you did on me. It'll be fine. And Billy knows to call uncle if he can't take it. Right?"

Sean looked to Billy, who slowly nodded, still looking a bit concerned.

Paul asked, "Should we uncuff him so he can sit up?"

"Nope. Sit on his face and let him show you how good he is with his tongue while you probe his cock," Sean said as he arranged the items next to the prone Billy.

Paul liked the idea of playing with Billy's cock and getting tongued while doing it. Jay had seemed to like it when Sean had done it to him, so he was looking forward to seeing what it felt like. But mostly, he was looking forward to playing with Billy's textbook-shaped, furiously red dick sticking out of his red pubes, and his smooth, scarlet-sacked balls.

"You okay with that?" Paul asked Billy.

Billy nodded.

"Don't matter what he's okay with, he belongs to me, and I say what he does and gets done to him," Sean said as he finished arranging the items next to Billy's hip. "Now, climb on and get busy, Paul."

Paul got into position over Billy so that his legs were comfortable with his ass directly over Billy's face, and so that he was also comfortable hovering over Billy's throbbing dick. The six inches of darkly red meat was almost weaving in the air with Billy's heartbeat. The head was deeply red, with nearly purple edges, and a round hole. The huge amount of pre-cum that had been produced over the last hour had soaked his short, sparse, red pubes.

Paul slid the tip of the little tube of lube into Billy's hole, then squeezed some into it. Then he stroked the urethral tube to push the lubricant deep into Billy's six-inch cock. Then he applied a drop of lubricant to the large, oval head of the probe.

"What the hell are these things called, anyway?" Paul asked, looking closely at the device.

"Bakes rosebud urethral dilator."

"Sounds like a medical device a doctor would use."

"I guess they're originally meant as a medical device, to stretch the urethra to make it easier to get a catheter in," Sean answered.

"Ah. Use the smaller ones, go larger, until the poor guy can take a catheter all the way in?" Paul asked as he worked the lube down Billy's urethra with the fingers of his other hand, enjoying touching and playing with Billy's hot, very hard dick.

It could easily be used as a basis for a textbook picture of a penis. The head was cone-shaped, tapered slightly, with slightly flared edges. It was almost exactly six inches long, straight, regular, and fairly smooth. The urethral tube wasn't as pronounced as Sean's or Jay's. Even his scrotum and balls seemed right out of a textbook on anatomy. The only thing that wasn't typical was the color of the sparse, short hairs at the base and that sprouted over the sack. Billy's thick, strong legs were pale, and the red hairs there were faint, sparse, and hard to see.

"Yeah, guess so," Sean answered.

"That's gotta hurt. Having a tube go all the way up there."

"Nope."

"You know?"

"Sure. Did it to Billy and he's done it to me."

"Real catheters?"

"Yeah."

"Where'd you get 'em?"

"My uncle gets them online. All kinds of places sell 'em."

"That's legal?"

"Sure. Guess so. You can buy 'em, anyway."

"What's it like?"

"Well, sorta the same, but when it gets in that deep, sorta past your prostate, it's a wild kind of pressure."

"What about when it... you know, goes in?"

"Feels weird. Nothing like a sounding does. There's just a wild, tickling kind of good feeling. For me and Billy, anyway. Maybe different for others. Wanna try sometime?"

The expression Paul wore didn't look like he was particularly interested.

"Don't you piss everywhere?"

"The end of the catheter has a valve. Some cheap ones just have a break-off. You can't not piss when one goes in, though."

"I'll pass," Paul said with a small snicker.

"Don't blame ya. I'll take a sounding anytime over just being cathed. But I've got a rubber tube that does the same thing but isn't hollow, so it works even better. But for now, stop wasting time and start working that thing in."

"Is it even gonna go?" Paul asked doubtfully.

Billy's opening wasn't small or tight, but it didn't look like the massive bead of the sounding rod was ever going to fit, even with the lube.

"Spread a little lube around the hole, and just keep working it in. Twist it, push, but not hard, and just keep working. Billy'll go nuts and probably leak a bunch of natural lube. If he says to stop, then stop. Otherwise, Billy, not a peep."

Billy nodded, grinning very widely. Sean leaned over to remove a large, black dildo from the overnight bag, lubed it, then waggled it as he spoke.

"Now, Paul, rock back a bit so Billy can use his tongue, and start working that thing in. And every time I hear Billy make a noise, I'm gonna give Victor a nudge."

Sean placed the dildo between Billy's legs, then wiggled it up against his anus.

Billy gasped, and his breath washed over Paul's anus, making it twitch. Paul lowered his ass and felt the first touch of a warm, wet tongue on it. He felt the tingling begin down there instantly as his body reacted to the new sensation.

"Oh, wow," Paul breathed.

"Nice, isn't it?" Sean asked as he spread Billy's legs and bent his knees, arranging them like frog's legs.

"Fucking nice!" Paul agreed, small shivers running up his thighs. "No way he can take that thing," he said as Sean nudged the big black dildo tightly against Billy's hole. Billy licked harder and probed. "Oh, God! That's so awesome!"

"Billy's good at it, for sure. And yeah, he's taken it before. He don't like it much, though."

Sean saw Paul's expression, and said, "Don't worry, he'll cry uncle if he has to. Now, get busy sliding that in his hole."

Paul let another series of shivers run through his thighs, inhaled then exhaled, then placed the oval bead against the slitted hole in Billy's dick.

Jay groaned softly. His body cried for attention, but all he could do was stretch out, or pull against the cuffs on his wrists and ankles. From where he lay, he could see Paul's ass on

Billy's face, but not his hole or Billy's tongue. But he could see Billy's dick in one of Paul's hands, and the wand in his other hand. And he could see Paul's cock hanging and dancing beneath him, as well as Sean's entire package as Sean lay with his ass aimed at Jay. Sean lay on his side with one leg up and that knee bent, making his brown hole exposed, and Jay stared at it and his balls and dick as well. The views made Jay's long cock flex in regular beats with his pulse, and pre-cum dribble from it, overflowing his navel. His head was dark red, the edges turning nearly purple. His body trembled and sweat shinned all over it. His breaths were short and rapid. The tingling pressure behind his scrotum was intense and growing. He'd never been so turned on before, even with all the sex and pleasure of the last few days.

The large, oval bead rested against the slit in the tip of Billy's head, and Paul applied a small amount of pressure as he twisted the rod. Billy's tongue worked in circles around his sphincter, making his body twitch at times.

Paul watched the tip of Billy's head indent as he pushed more, twisting the rod, trying to insert it.

"How hard do I push?" Paul asked.

"As hard as it takes. Go slow, don't rush it, but it if hurts or something, Billy'll let ya know," Sean said.

The tip of Paul's tongue poked out between his lips as he worked the oval bead against the tip of Billy's head. The indentation grew deeper as Paul pushed more, and suddenly the oval bead spread the hole open and Billy's spread legs quivered. Paul felt Billy's hot breath on his wet hole and heard the soft moan. Then he watched as Sean pushed the huge, black dildo against Billy's tight, pink asshole. Billy's legs tensed and his back arched, and his tongue dove into Paul's rear, opening his sphincter and probing inside, making Paul gasp.

The opening of Billy's cock slowly spread around the bead, like lips around a cock. Paul was fascinated at the sight. He applied a little more pressure. The soft skin around the opening stretched around the bead and it slid in deeper. With a twist, it popped inside. Billy shuddered silently and waves ran along his thighs.

"I don't believe it," Paul gasped at the obvious bulge just where the two coronal edges met under Billy's head. "I can see it making a huge bump under his head!"

"Cool, huh?" Sean asked, grinning.

"Fucking wild!" Paul agreed. "That doesn't hurt?"

Billy's tongue roamed over both cheeks of Paul's ass, left to right and back, but he was silent, using his tongue to demonstrate a negative shake of his head.

"He didn't cry uncle, so keep going," Sean said, smiling.

Paul's cock twitched powerfully and a drop of pre-cum began stretching downward from it toward Billy's chest. From the other side of the bed, Jay saw the string forming and lengthen, and he ached to be able to reach it. He'd experienced a lot of new and intense sensations over the last week, but this prolonged state of excitement and the sight of all that was being done in front of him as he lay restrained was pushing his body and mind even further than before. The pool of fluid in his navel now ran over and flowed down his side as more pre-cum joined it. His body was constantly trembling now, shining with sweat, and his breaths were nearly labored. He could do nothing to stop the soft groans with each breath.

Billy had to work hard to prevent himself from making any noises. The bead had pushed him to his limits as it had stretched his hole open at first. It had been almost the most intense moment of his life. He had taken the same bead before, but only after some of the smaller ones first, working up to the largest. Taking the largest without that stretching was intense and nearly so painful he had cried uncle to make it stop. But he had persevered, and now it had gained entry and was stretching the inside of his cock, sending powerful waves of pleasure and pain through his cock and up his spine. His body shivered, and his chest shook from the effort to maintain his stationary position. The urge to pump his hips was strong. All he could do was work his tongue in Paul's smooth ass crack and into his tight, virgin hole.

Sean was intensely turned on. He and Billy had done many things together, but watching the inexperienced Paul probe Billy's little cock with the massive probe had his cock throbbing wildly. He stroked himself several times, gathered up the pre-cum at his hole with two fingers, and fed it to Jay, who groaned loudly, earning him a grin from Paul and Sean.

"He's gonna explode when we get to him," Sean said, grinning wickedly at Jay.

Paul laughed softly, then gave Jay a long, gentle look. Jay felt himself tremble even more. His body yearned to feel someone touching him in any way.

"Back to Billy for now," Sean said, running a hand up and down Billy's thigh as his other kept the pressure on Billy's hole with the large dildo.

Paul nodded, then looked back at the silver wand in Billy's dick. He let go of the wand to allow it to slide deeper, but he ended up letting go of it entirely and with no movement of the wand.

"It's too big to go on its own," Sean said. "You'll have to help it. Gently and slow."

Paul nodded, then gave the wand a little assistance. It began moving downward, the bulge visibly moving down Billy's urethra. Paul was amazed, and his cock pulsed again, severing the long string of pre-cum so that it fell onto Billy's chest. Billy felt it, and knew what it was, and wished that he could wipe it up with a finger and place that finger between his lips and Paul's hole, licking it clean and tickling Paul there with it at the same time. But all he could do was lick and probe Paul's dark, tight hole. He loved that he was licking a hole that had never felt it before, and that had never had anything inside of it. Billy shoved his tongue into it, and Paul shivered slightly and inhaled sharply.

"Geeze!"

"Told ya, Billy knows what he's doing!" Sean said gleefully.

"No kiddin!"

Paul gave a little pressure to the wand, moving it deeper into Billy's dick, and watching the progress of the sizable lump visible in his urethra. Billy's body tensed again, and his hot breath washed over Paul's wet ass crack, making his body tingle again.

"Not even halfway yet," Sean said, reaching out to play with Billy's balls with his free hand, his other still maintaining the pressure on Billy's hole with Victor the dildo.

"I don't know how he stands it," Paul said, pushing the wand deeper.

"He's had it before," Sean said, rolling Billy's balls in his hand.

Billy licked upward from Paul's hole, then down along his

taint, finally taking one of his balls in his mouth. Paul groaned and grimaced.

"That's fucking cool," he said, then pushed the wand gently.

Billy moaned around the nut in his mouth. Sean pushed Victor against Billy's pink hole, pushing the soft skin there inward noticeably, the hole not opening to allow the large thing in. Paul groaned in pleasure at what was being done to him, what he was doing to Billy, and at what he was seeing being done to Billy. Another string of pre-cum began hanging downward toward Billy's nearly smooth, well-muscled chest.

Jay had been watching the wand disappear into Billy's dick, inch by inch. The sight was intense and fascinating, and he couldn't look away, except in short stints to take in what Billy was doing to Paul's ass and short glances at Sean's ass. All three of them were buff and well-muscled to differing degrees, and with different hair and skin tones. Jay couldn't ask for a hotter sight. His body told him that any hotter a sight would result in his achieving an orgasm.

It was the first time Billy had something pushing at his anus while a rod was inserted in his cock. It was intensely pleasurable, and the threat of Victor spreading him open too was making him quiver all over, sweat, and his breath come fast.

Paul wiggled the wand experimentally, and Billy let out a groan. Sean smiled and pushed Victor against Billy's hole. Billy's pink hole was being pushed inward, and he was sure the very tip of the large dildo was beginning to spread it open.

Jay's body was covered in sweat, and his breath came rapid gasps. Every muscle vibrated, and his groin and hips tensed and released in a slow, repetitive timing that he found irresistible. It was doing something to him that he had never felt before. His balls became nearly numb, and his cock felt as if it were stretching the skin covering it. The slow pulsing below them was nearly the same as when he was cumming, but nothing was being done to his aching cock. Nevertheless, he felt as if an enormous orgasm was growing close. He whimpered in extreme pleasure with each breath, quivering all over.

Paul twisted the rod slowly, applying light pressure, and the large, visible lump moved down the shaft, now nearly three-quarters of the way to the base.

"Will it go all the way?" Paul asked.

"It'll go 'till Billy says to stop," Sean said.

Paul gently pushed the wand deeper. The lump moved further down. He pushed more, but there was real resistance.

"I think that's as far as it goes," Paul said.

"Push just a little harder," Sean said.

"I don't think I should," Paul answered.

Billy was panting into Paul's ass, licking and probing with his tongue, and enjoying being the first one to do so to it. That was exciting enough, but having that same inexperienced boy probing him, and with the largest one at that, was incredible. And having Sean pushing Victor slowly into him was almost too much, even for the well-experienced Billy. But he wanted more, and Paul seemed hesitant to give him more of the large sounding wand. He pushed his hips upward.

"See, he wants more," Sean said. "Just hold it still, let him push up for it next time. "

Paul did so, and when Billy pushed his hips upward, he drove the wand deeper into himself.

"When he drops his hips, let the wand go so you don't pull it out," Sean said.

When Billy's hips fell back to the bed, Paul held the wand steady but didn't let it come out any. As Billy pushed upward again, Paul held the wand firmly, and ever so slowly, Billy fed the wand deeper into himself, then dropped his hips back onto the bed. Soon, Billy stopped doing so and lay still.

Having the largest probe already in him, and the enormous dildo beginning to spread him open was incredible. He had gotten the probe as deep as it could go, and slowly moved his hips in tiny increments, sliding the bead inside of himself.

"That's as far as he wants it," Sean said. "Twist it, like you did for me, while he fucks himself with the wand."

Paul held the rod steady as Billy began working it in and out of himself very slowly. Billy's legs quivered, waves rolling along the soft skin of the insides of them. Paul's cock dribbled more pre-cum onto Billy's chest. Paul moaned softly, watching the wand sliding in Billy's urethra, gently twisting it. Billy trembled violently and let out another soft moan. Sean pushed against his hole with the large, black dildo, and Billy felt his sphincter begin to open around the end of it. Paul groaned and began rocking back and forth, amplifying the motion of Billy's tongue on his sphincter.

Jay's cock was now purple, wet with a nearly constant stream of pre-cum that formed a large puddle around his navel and a trail down his side. His entire body trembled as he worked his hips, using muscles deep inside himself he'd never paid any attention to before. The new sensation of using those muscles was pushing him closer to an actual handless orgasm.

"Hold the wand with your teeth and bob up and down, like you're blowing him," Sean said to Paul.

Paul did so, and rested his weight on his hands. Billy's rapid breaths began making whining noises, and Sean pushed the dildo into him further, until the edges of the dildo's head held Billy's pink hole open.

The sight made Paul groan and shiver, and his cock pulsate repeatedly, slapping Billy's chest. A string of sticky fluid connected Billy's chest and Paul's cock, stretching as his cock bobbed upward, making a wet slapping sound as the head slapped Billy's chest.

Billy could barely hold back more moans as Victor began entering him. Because it had been pushing against him for some time, his hole had begun spreading for it, and there was almost no pain, but there was a lot of pleasure. Especially as the soft edges of the head entered. With that, and the large wand deep in his urethra, his body trembled powerfully. Paul's balls in his mouth when he wasn't licking the virgin hole, and his nice cock drooling onto his chest and slapping against it, all was incredibly pleasurable.

As Paul pulled the wand upward a small amount, cloudy fluid poured from the hole. Billy gasped around Paul's balls, and Sean pushed Victor further into Billy's pink hole. Paul groaned at the sight, and at what he was doing to Billy himself, as well as what Billy's mouth was doing to his ass and nuts. Sean stroked himself a few times again, and again wiped up the pre-cum the few strokes produced and then let Jay suck it off his fingers.

This was too much for Jay. He had been pumping his hips in that irresistible rhythm for long minutes now, and his body had borne all it could, and with a heavy grunt, he began having an orgasm that wracked his body. He strained against the cuffs on his wrist and ankles as his body twisted, trying to curl up over his aching and throbbing balls, then his back arcing the other way, thrusting his hips upward. A few droplets sprayed out of his dick to land midway up his chest, then with another loud grunt that got the attention of the other three boys, he began spurting semen in a low arc that ended on his own face. It was nearly a constant stream, broken only momentarily. At first, the other boys thought he was urinating on himself with some force, but as they saw that the stream was white and thick, and landed with audible plops and splashes that spread across his face, they were stunned. Jay groaned loudly again and again, low, deep, loud grunts that matched the timing of the short pauses in the long stream of white.

Jay's back continued to whip his body back and forth between trying to curl over his nearly painful groin to thrusting his hips high off the surface of the bed. The chains of the cuffs rattled loudly, but were nearly drowned by his cries or orgasmic ecstasy. It was the most intense pleasure he had felt yet, and was so strong it caused pain to rise between his balls and his cock. His sack was merely a small, curved, wrinkled bump between his tensing and stammering thighs as they emptied through his long, thick, pulsating cock.

The long, almost constant stream of semen first shot onto his face, but lower with each pulsation, the thick fluid now splashing onto his neck, then his heaving chest, then his straining belly. As his body locked upright, his ass inches above the bed, his straining cock throbbed a last few times, oozing thick, almost chunky cum out just far enough to fall from his dark-purple head, overflowing his already pre-cum filled navel and rolling down his side in a lumpy white trail.

Suddenly, as if he had been struck, Jay's body fell onto the bed and his breath whooshed from him. A final wave of trembling muscles and he lay still, except for his heavy panting. His eyes were closed and his expression empty and slack.

"That looked like it hurt!" Sean said, laughing.

"Fucking awesome!" Billy crooned.

Paul said, "He never even got touched. How'd he shoot off?"

"He was pushing his hips the right way. And was really turned on. It can be done. Guess he learned how," Sean answered.

"You can really cum without at least jerking it?"

"If you're turned on enough, and work the muscles down there the right way. I've read about it."

"Fuckin' amazing!" Paul said, looking at Jay's cum-covered face and front. "I'm not wasting that."

"So, go ahead. I can't let go of Victor, or I'll have to start over. I'll have some fun with the stick while you clean up Jay," Sean said.

Billy let out a loud groan, so Sean applied more pressure to Victor, sliding it further into him. Paul watched a full inch of the massive dildo invade Billy's pink hole. Billy's cock tensed and throbbed, forcing the wand upward nearly an inch. His body shook and his balls retracted, the sack wrinkling up around them.

Billy was close to cumming, but he didn't want to yet. The wand deep in his urethra, Victor entering him, Paul's virgin ass and his balls to lick, and watching Jay explode all brought him perilously close to orgasm.

Paul crawled to Jay. He was shining with sweat, and breathing deeply and slowly. Paul leaned down to kiss his lips, where some cum had landed. After the soft, gentle, salty kiss, Paul began licking and kissing all of Jay's face, cleaning away the thick, warm cum. It was heavily musky and slightly bitter. Paul moved slowly around Jay's face, cleaning carefully and slowly, before slowly moving down to his neck, his chest, his belly, and lower, taking quite a while to clean the large pool in and around his navel. Then Paul took his time at licking and cleaning the soft, thick cock, milking it with his hand to get the last drops from it.

Meanwhile, Sean began working the spike inside of Billy again, making him twist and heave. Sean kept Victor inside Billy's pink pucker, moving it ever so gently.

Paul kissed Jay again, softly and gently, one hand cradling the back of his head, the other over his still hammering heart. They kissed for long minutes before taking a break. When Paul turned back to look at Billy and Sean, they were looking at him closely.

"What?" Paul asked, turning red.

"You're really into him, ain't ya?"

Paul darkened even further, trying to hide the grin that only grew instead.

"Don't bug it. If you do, that's great. And it's obvious you do," Sean said softly.

Paul laughed softly, still grinning and red-faced. He shrugged.

"Well, you ready to get back to working Billy here?" Sean asked with a nod at the handle of the wand he held, slowly twisting and moving it.

"He still hasn't gotten off?" Paul asked, stunned.

Billy's cock was amazingly red, the skin behind the head puffy, his balls tucked up so tightly that they were no longer even visible. A sheen of sweat covered his entire body, and the shudders wracking him were clearly visible.

"Nope. Not yet," Sean said, grinning wickedly. "Not that he didn't try a couple of times."

Billy had indeed tried to reach orgasm, but Sean's mastery had prevented it. He had tried to cause an orgasm by thrusting his hips, the way Jay had, but had been unsuccessful. He was so excited that he couldn't think clearly. The sensations of Victor in him while the rod stroked its way through his urethra was one of the most intense combinations he'd ever felt.

Paul grinned, then moved to take back the sounding wand from Sean once he was back in position over Billy. As soon as he began moving the wand again, Billy began licking from the back of his sack up over his hole, then over his balls and cock and then back over his hole. The few black hairs around Paul's hole were plastered flat by Billy's saliva, and his dark hole quivered in the middle of them as Billy's tongue licked over it.

As Paul moved the wand up and down, turning it from time to time, the bead pushed cloudy fluid out of Billy's small hole. Paul licked it away, liking the almost salty and almost sweet flavor of Billy's pre-cum. He didn't know why he liked Billy's red hair and pubes, or his average six inches of meat, but it was very attractive to Paul and turned him on quite a bit. But Jay's lean body, his large, thick cock, and Jay in general, was far more attractive to him.

Paul began stroking the wand, and the massive bead on the end of it, through Billy's average cock, the large bead showing clearly in the urethra beneath his dick as it moved back into view before it disappeared again behind Billy's scrotum. When the wand came mostly up the short cock, a small amount of cloudy fluid washed out of the hole around the stem of the wand, and Paul gladly licked it up.

Billy's cock flexed, and the head was now almost entirely purple.

"You getting close again?" Sean asked.

Billy grunted, "Close!"

Sean pushed Victor deeper, making Billy grunt and his cock swell in Paul's hand. More pre-cum washed up, more than previously, and Paul cleaned it away with his lips and tongue.

"Pull it out, slow," Sean said to Paul.

Paul began withdrawing the rod, a large trail of pre-cum rolling down the top of his head and into the web between Paul's thumb and finger. Billy shuddered violently as the large, oval bead popped out of his red hole, creating another trail of pre-cum.

"Suck him off," Sean said. "Both of you."

They began doing so, and the sounds of eager blow-jobs filled the room. Paul was able to push his nose into Billy's sack, taking all of his six inches. Billy easily took all of Paul's six inches, and Paul's smallish balls slapped against his nose or forehead as he bobbed upward.

Both began moaning deeply, and Billy nearly screamed as Victor was pushed further into him. His cock flexed in Paul's mouth and then filled his mouth with pre-cum. Sean began moving Victor in short strokes, moving it through Billy's tight, now red hole. Billy squirmed and shivered, panting around Paul's cock. He was experienced, so his tongue washed every inch of Paul's cock as it slid through his lips.

In mere moments, Paul's balls began pulling upward and into him, and Billy tasted the large flow of salty pre-cum. Paul felt that pressure beneath him expand and grow, seeming to fill him up from there to the top of his head in pulsing waves. His toes curled almost painfully, and his ankles popped as his muscles sought some kind of relief from the incredible pleasure and pressure.

Paul grunted, then gulped Billy's cock as far as he could. They both groaned as Paul began pushing himself deeply into Billy's mouth. Paul's body was nearly tortured by another orgasm, and it being an oral one, and the practiced and knowledgeable Billy working his cock professionally, it was the most intense one yet, torturing his body and mind with levels of pleasure he had never felt before. He barely managed to continue sucking and licking Billy's cock as his body tensed and vibrated strongly with the mere beginning of the orgasm. He forgot Billy's cock and balls in his hands as his vision darkened and his breath stopped. He held on, shaking, grunting, as the orgasm turned his balls inside-out, over and over.

Billy was experienced and swallowed it as fast as Paul provided it, sucking and licking. Paul's skin prickled and his mind went blank, filled with only the blindingly powerful throes of the most intense orgasm of his life so far. His body locked rigid, his breath caught, his eyes crushed closed, his balls pushing thick, heavy cum through him. Paul was lost. The suction that Billy kept providing, and his tongue working the sensitive head, put Paul somewhere he had never gone before.

Sean watched, enthralled, as Paul's body locked rigid and trembled like an earthquake shook the entire planet around him. No breath passed through him, and the expression on his face resembled one he had seen on someone who had just broken his leg.

Finally, Paul realized he was alive, and that the things his mind was telling him that his body was feeling were real, and not some kind of unbelievably pleasurable torture. The pressure between his balls and ass lessened, and the pleasure that Billy's mouth and tongue were giving him increased even further. With a gasp, he pulled himself from Billy's mouth and rolled onto his side, grabbing his sore and hot cock and balls.

"Holy fuck!" he groaned, shaking, eyes closed, curled around his middle, panting for breath.

Sean grinned at him, then turned to Billy and began licking up from the base of Billy's dick to the very tip, which was now purple. Billy bucked as Sean's lips closed over his head and he sucked momentarily. Sean kept moving Victor gently, making him writhe.

After all the play and sexual tension, Billy was preparing for an extreme orgasm. The pulsing pleasure between his balls and where Victor spread him open grew, washing through his entire body. Muscles began tensing everywhere. He grunted a warning.

Sean stopped and then gave Billy an evil grin. Billy grinned back, knowing it wasn't going to happen this time, either. Sean began slowly pulling Victor from him. Billy exhaled loudly when the pressure of the massive thing finally left him, then he shuddered again with another heavy sigh.

Sean stretched out next to the still cuffed Billy, sharing a knowing grin with him. Sean ground his erection against Billy's thigh, spreading his pre-cum on Billy's pale skin. He traced his finger over Billy's nipples and belly, often following the curves and bulges of the well-defined muscles all over his body. The faint, red hairs were few and light, and ordinarily hard to see, except that now they were dark and plastered to his skin with sweat. Billy shivered, his cock throbbing with his pulse, his balls tight in their wrinkled, nearly scarlet sack.

"Can I unlock his cuffs?" Paul asked from behind him.

"Sure, if you want," Sean said, moving to get the key from the overnight bag.

After a few moments, he checked to make sure Jay and Paul weren't looking, then winked at Billy as he held up the small key momentarily, then closed his fist hiding it, and asked, "Billy? Did you pick up the key?"

Billy moaned, "Uhhh…"

Sean groaned, "Oh, shit."

"No way!" Paul exclaimed loudly in disbelief, whipping his head around. "You guys really forgot the fucking key?

Sean shrugged at him, grinning.

"You dumb-asses!" Paul said angrily.

"Don't worry. We'll figure out something," Sean said.

"There's a hacksaw in the shed," Jay said hopefully.

"We'll get 'em out of 'em later, then," Sean said, then closed the bag, dropping the key inside of it secretly.

"Then we'll kick your ass," Paul said, then arranged himself next to Jay, pulling him into a hug. Paul brushed the sweat-damp hair from Jay's forehead and cradled his head with his arm. They stared into each other's eyes for a few moments, then kissed softly and deeply.

Paul couldn't remember feeling so happy and satisfied. Not just sexually, but emotionally. Holding Jay felt right and perfect. Warm, soft, fuzzy… just wonderful. He'd always wanted to feel something special with someone, and now he knew he was. He couldn't wait to give Jay what he wanted, to make him as happy and satisfied as he felt at that moment. He was looking forward to finding Jay's limits, and sometimes going a little further, just to keep him sharp and on edge. The prospect of doing those things to Jay made him feel as if he'd found his reason for existence. He knew he was falling for Jay, and only hoped that Jay might feel something for him, too.

Jay was thinking nearly the exact same things as they held and kissed each other. The comfort and feeling of safety and security in Paul's arms was everything he'd hoped he would experience someday. Even the smell of Paul made him feel good. His strong arms around him were like walls enclosing him, protecting him from outside dangers. He felt as if nothing could harm him right then. And he knew that Paul would push him as far as he wanted, and sometimes a little further, just to keep him on his toes. The thought of giving Paul pleasure gave him tingles of anticipation. He shuddered with the expectations of their times together.

Sean saw how tenderly and gently Paul and Jay held each other and knew what it meant. He wondered if what he felt for Billy was the same or not. He doubted it. He cared for Billy a great deal, considered him his best friend, and more, and enjoyed what they did together, but he didn't have the same kind of need or desire for tenderness for Billy. He loved making Billy sweat and groan, shiver and shudder, and making him wait as long as possible for release, but they rarely held each other or hugged. They never kissed after, only before, just to warm up, and rarely during. He loved hurting Billy, and he knew Billy loved being hurt, which made it even better to hurt him. He didn't like really hurting Billy, only giving him what he liked and wanted.

Sean looked at Billy, who was also looking at Paul and how he held Jay. Billy's expression told Sean that Billy wanted that, too. When Billy looked at Sean and saw him looking at him, he blushed furiously and grinned.

"Not what we got, is it?" Billy asked.

"Sure isn't. You like what we got?"

"Hell yes! Wouldn't trade it for anything!" Billy said emphatically. He looked back at Paul and Jay, then back at Sean again, then with a small loss of his smile, said, "Maybe except for what they got."

Sean nodded, his grin also weakening a little. "They'll want to be with just each other next. Probably as soon as we get back home, ya know?" he said a bit sadly.

"Well, until we find someone like that, we got each other."

"Yeah. And we still got tonight and tomorrow with 'em," Sean said, his grin returning.

"A lot to teach in that time, too," Billy agreed, his grin also returning.